P9-EMP-601

CRAB & SNAIL

THE INVISIBLE WHALE

For Chris and Joe, my favorite surfers—B.F.

For my mom and dad—J.C.

HarperAlley is an imprint of HarperCollins Publishers.

Crab and Snail: The Invisible Whale
Text copyright © 2022 by Beth Ferry
Art copyright © 2022 by Jared Chapman

All rights reserved. Manufactured in Italy. No part of this book may be used or reproduced
in any manner whatsoever without written permission except in the case of brief quotations
embodied in critical articles and reviews. For information address HarperCollins Children's
Books, a division of HarperCollins Publishers, 195 Broadway, New York, NY 10007.
www.harpercollinschildrens.com

ISBN 978-0-06-296213-3 (p-o-b)
ISBN 978-0-06-296214-0 (pbk.)

Typography by Chelsea C. Donaldson
21 22 23 24 25   RTLO   10 9 8 7 6 5 4 3 2 1
❖
First Edition

CRAB & SNAIL

THE INVISIBLE WHALE

by Beth Ferry

pictures by Jared Chapman

HARPER alley

An Imprint of HarperCollinsPublishers

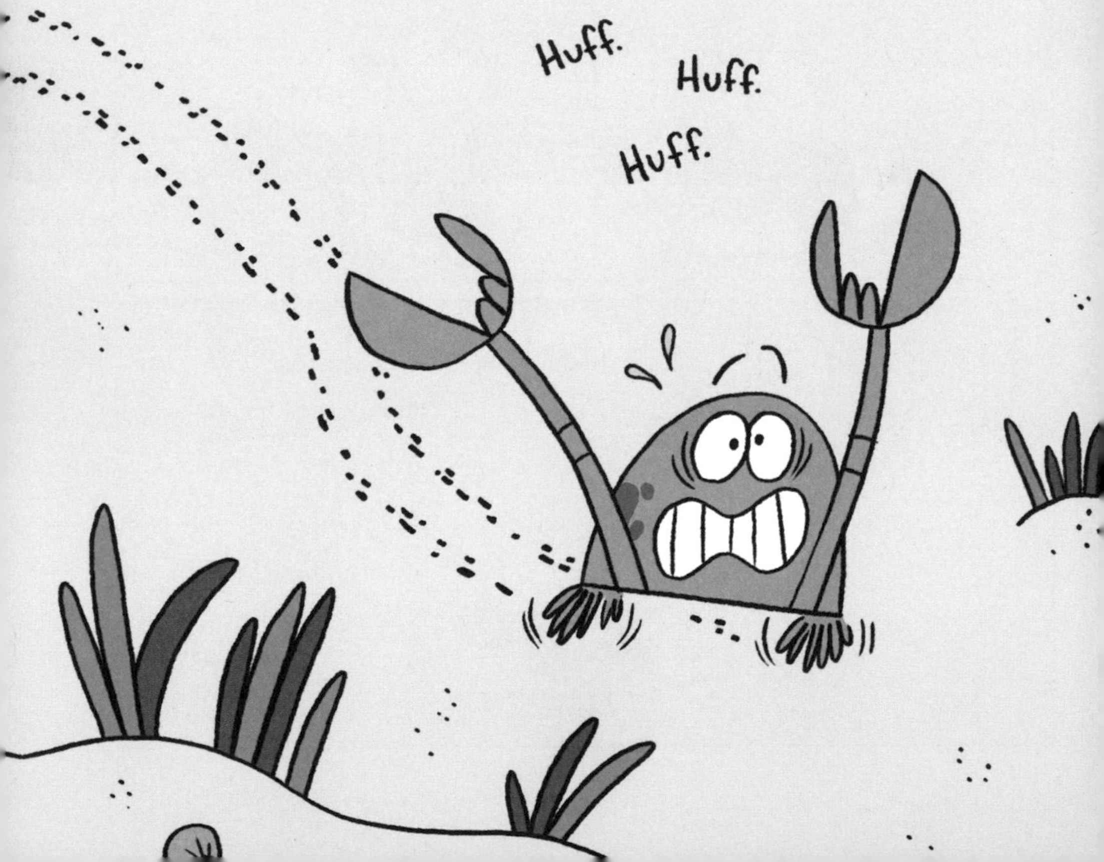
Huff.
Huff.
Huff.

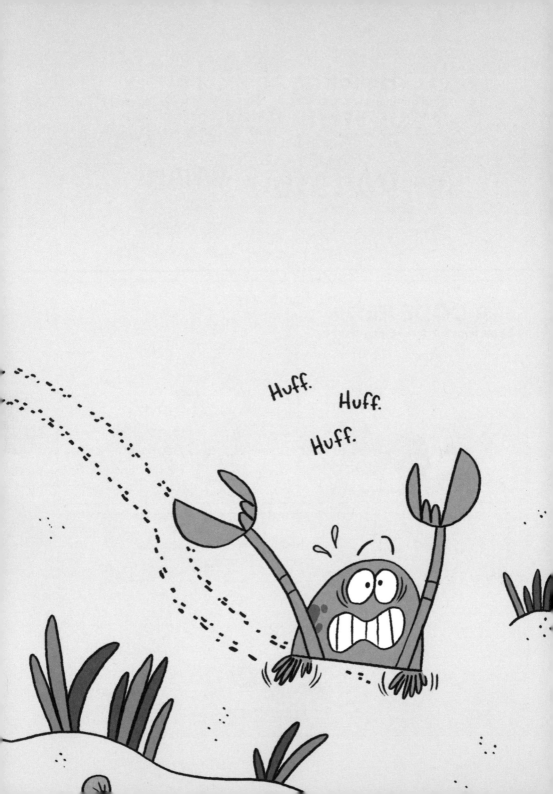

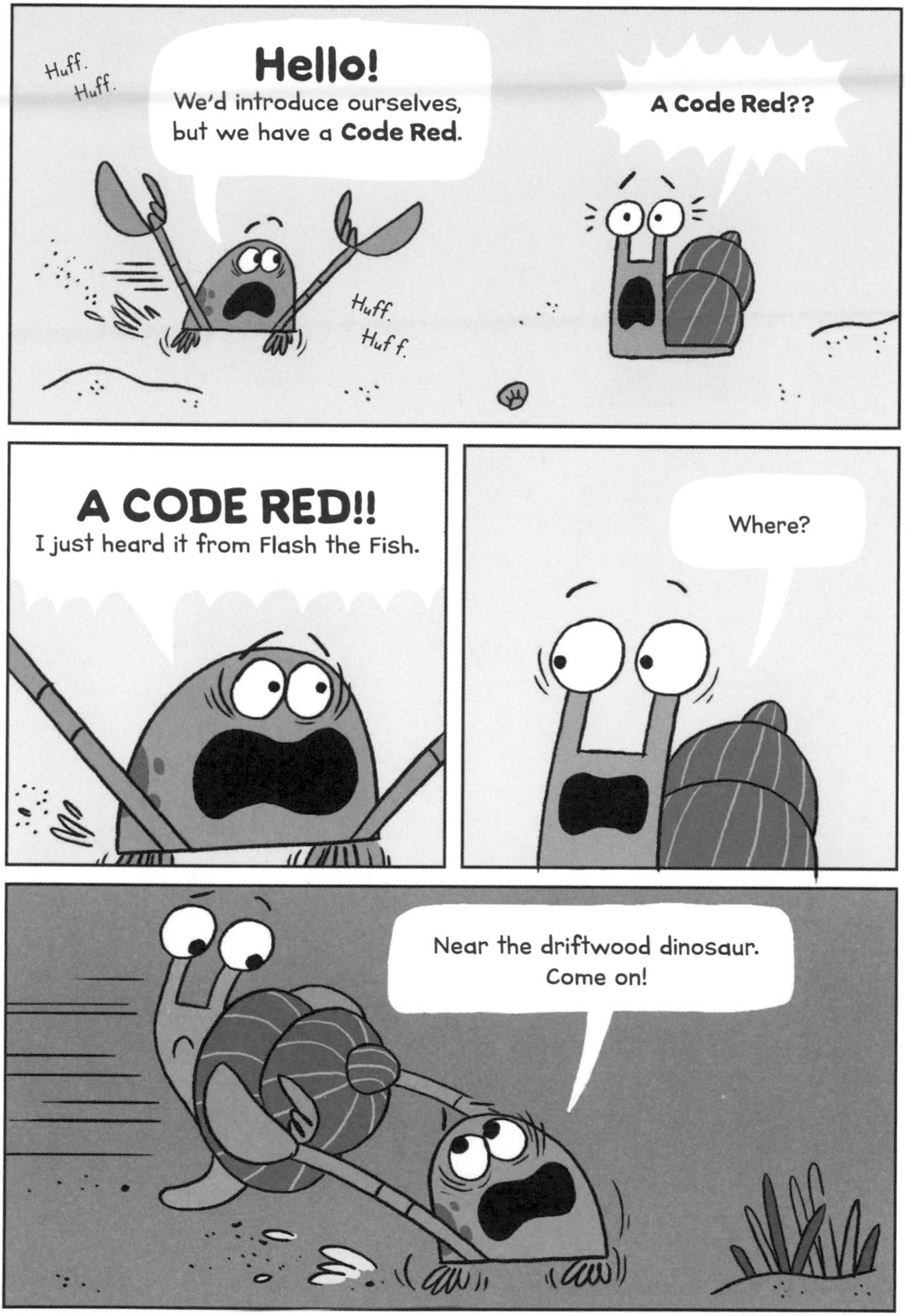

Huff. Huff.
Hello! We'd introduce ourselves, but we have a Code Red.
Huff. Huff.
A Code Red??
A CODE RED!! I just heard it from Flash the Fish.
Where?
Near the driftwood dinosaur. Come on!

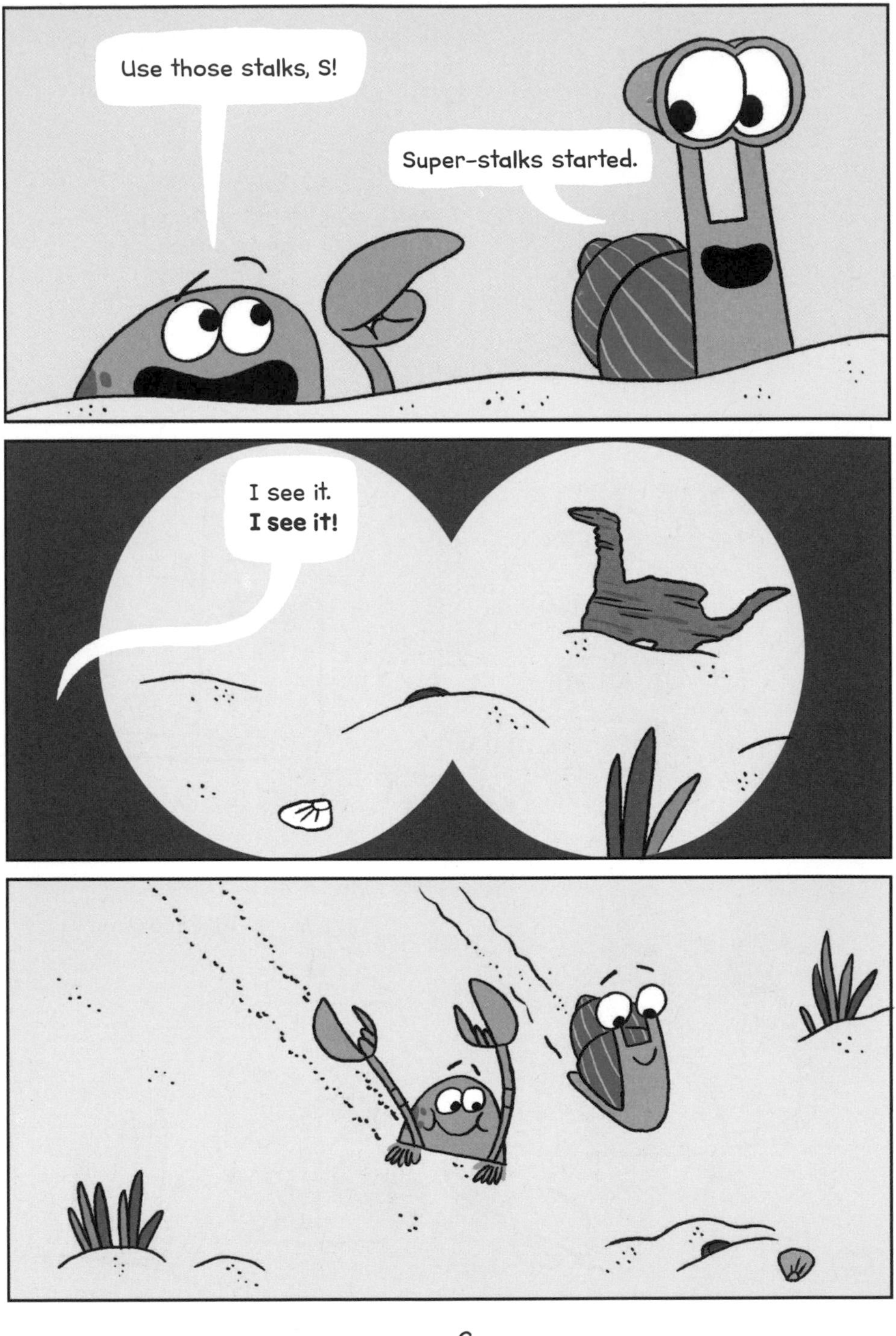
Use those stalks, S!
Super-stalks started.
I see it.
I see it!

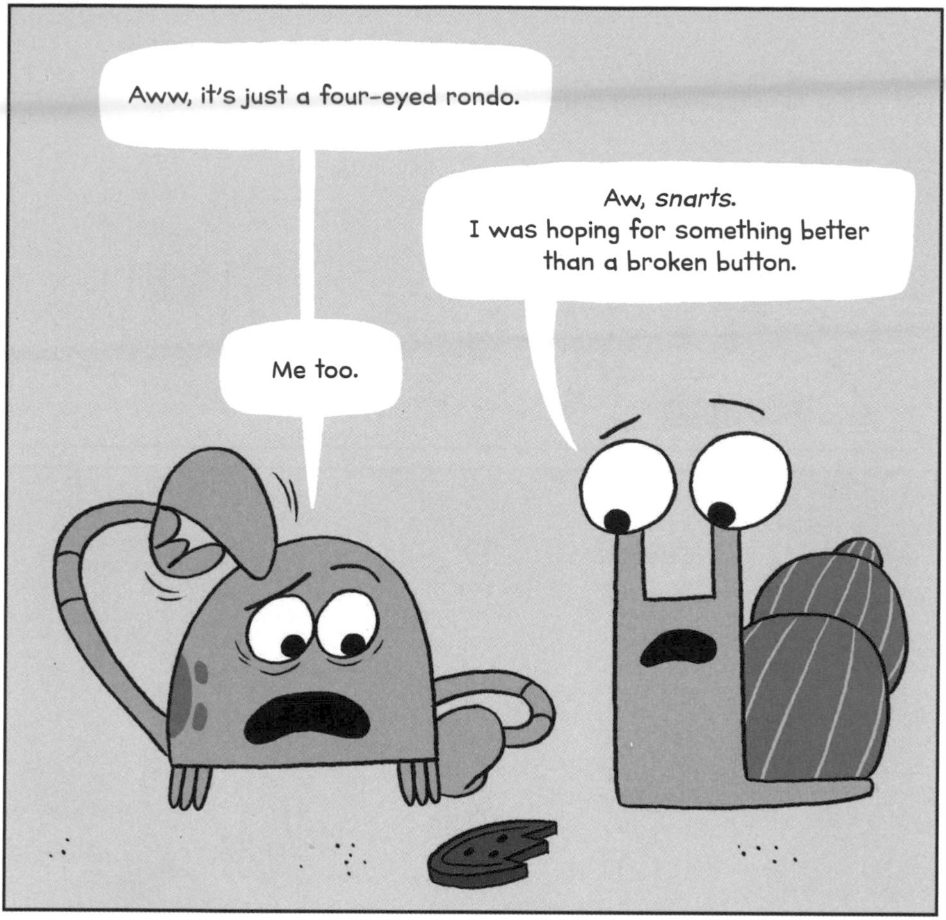
Aww, it's just a four-eyed rondo.
Aw, *snarts*. I was hoping for something better than a broken button.
Me too.

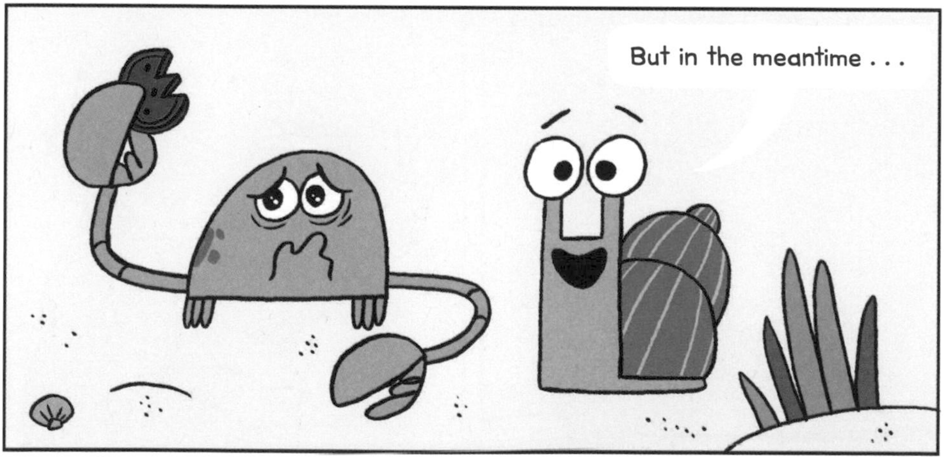
But in the meantime . . .

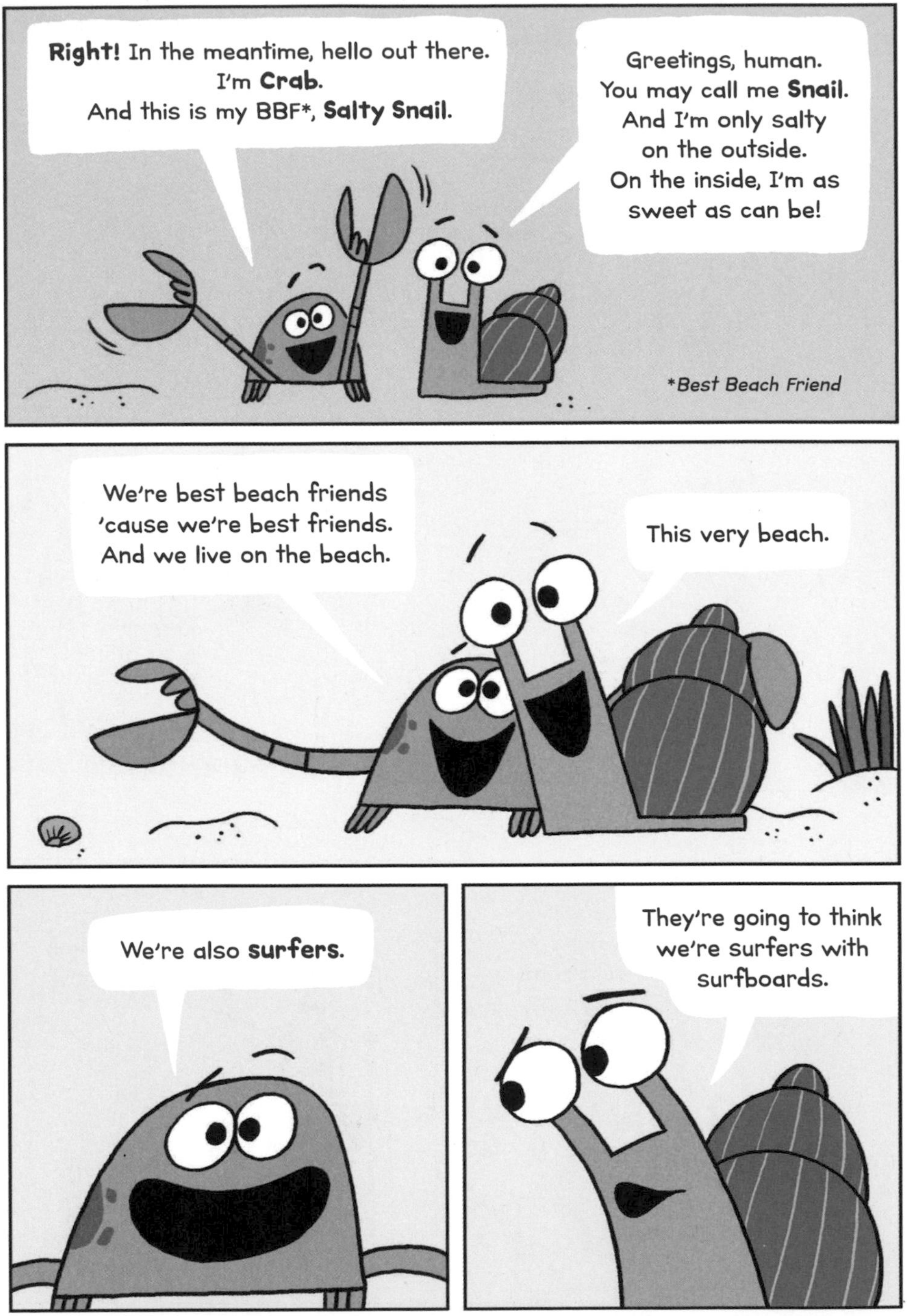
Right! In the meantime, hello out there. I'm **Crab**. And this is my BBF*, **Salty Snail**.
Greetings, human. You may call me **Snail**. And I'm only salty on the outside. On the inside, I'm as sweet as can be!
*Best Beach Friend
We're best beach friends 'cause we're best friends. And we live on the beach.
This very beach.
We're also **surfers**.
They're going to think we're surfers with surfboards.

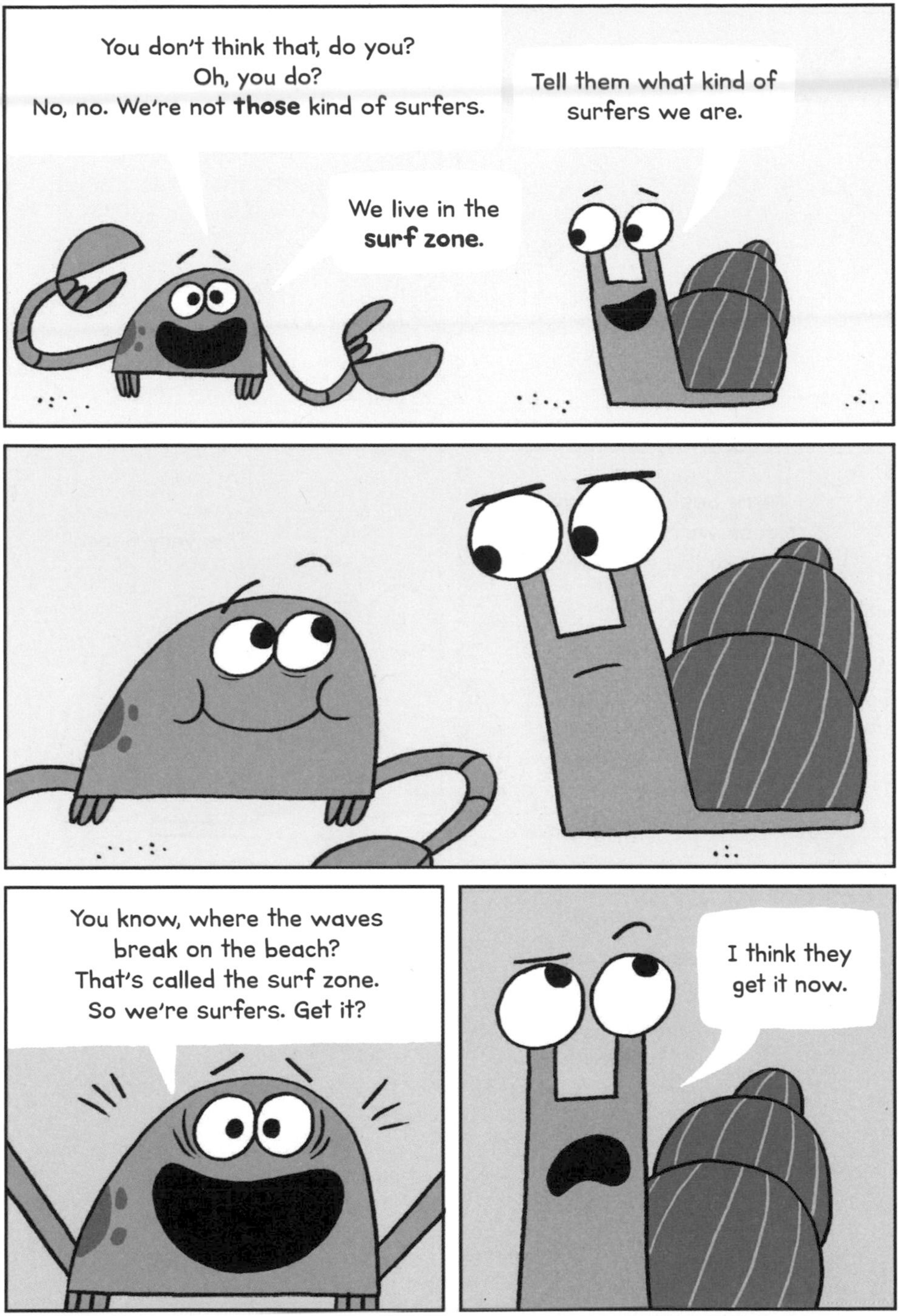
You don't think that, do you?
Oh, you do?
No, no. We're not **those** kind of surfers.
Tell them what kind of surfers we are.
We live in the **surf zone.**
You know, where the waves break on the beach?
That's called the surf zone.
So we're surfers. Get it?
I think they get it now.

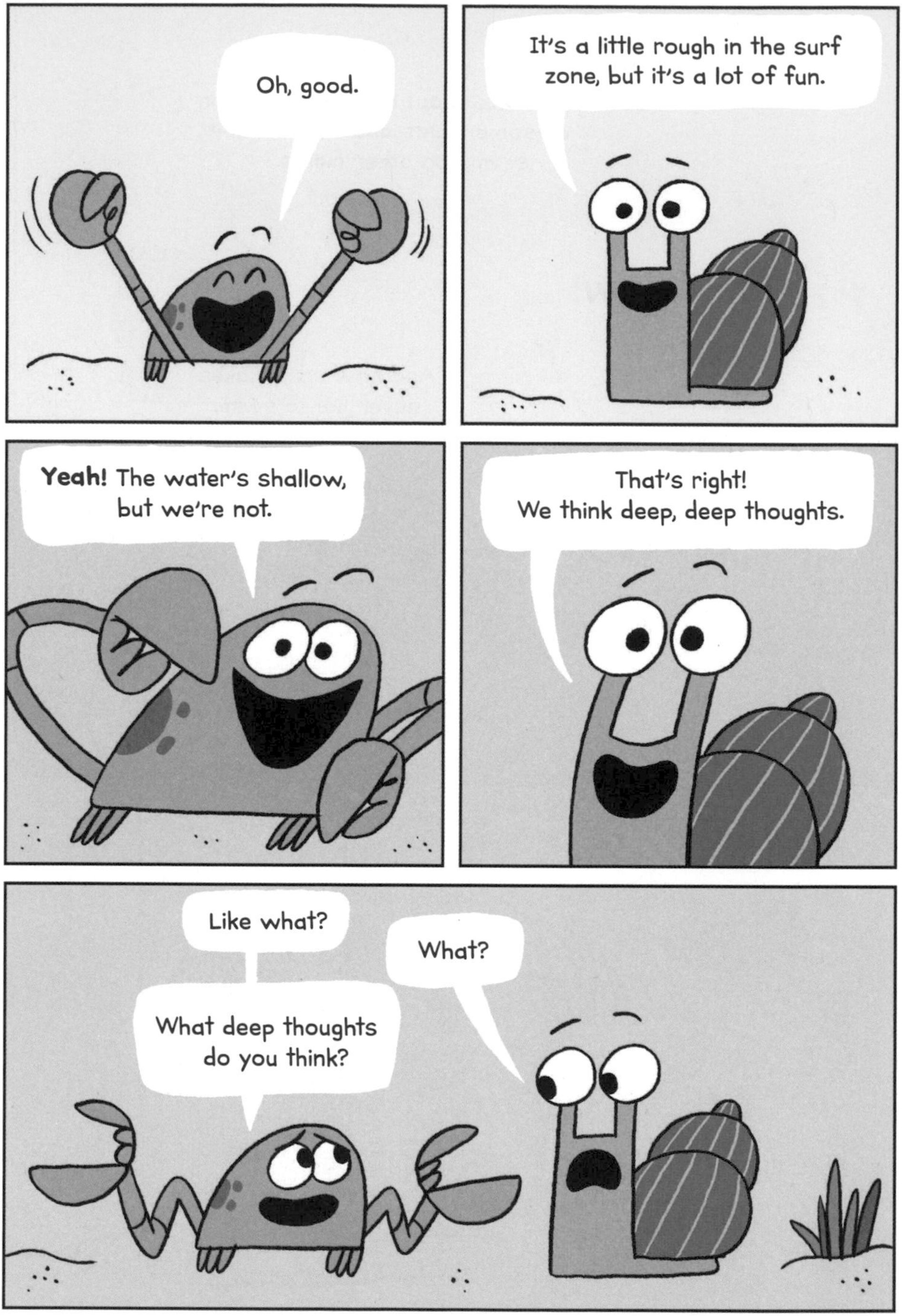
Oh, good.
It's a little rough in the surf zone, but it's a lot of fun.
Yeah! The water's shallow, but we're not.
That's right! We think deep, deep thoughts.
Like what?
What deep thoughts do you think?
What?

Well, I think about how big the moon is on some nights and how small it seems on other nights.
Wow!
And how snowflakes never get to swim.
Cool!

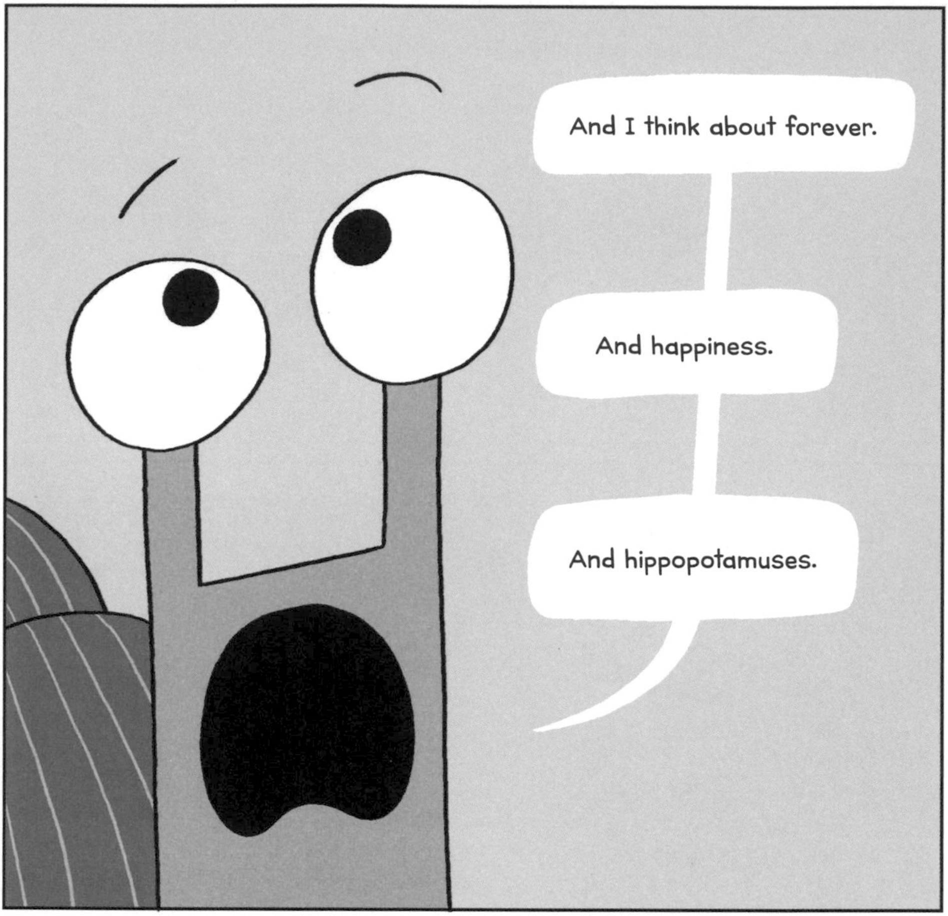
And I think about forever.
And happiness.
And hippopotamuses.

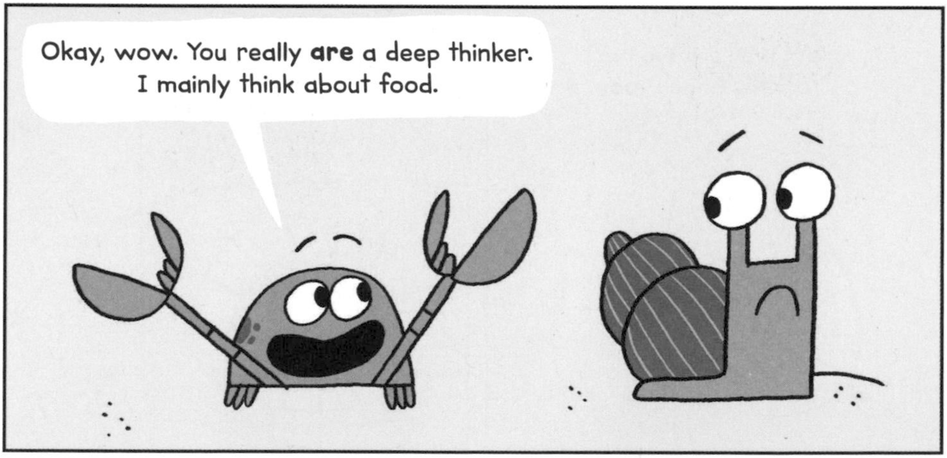
Okay, wow. You really **are** a deep thinker. I mainly think about food.

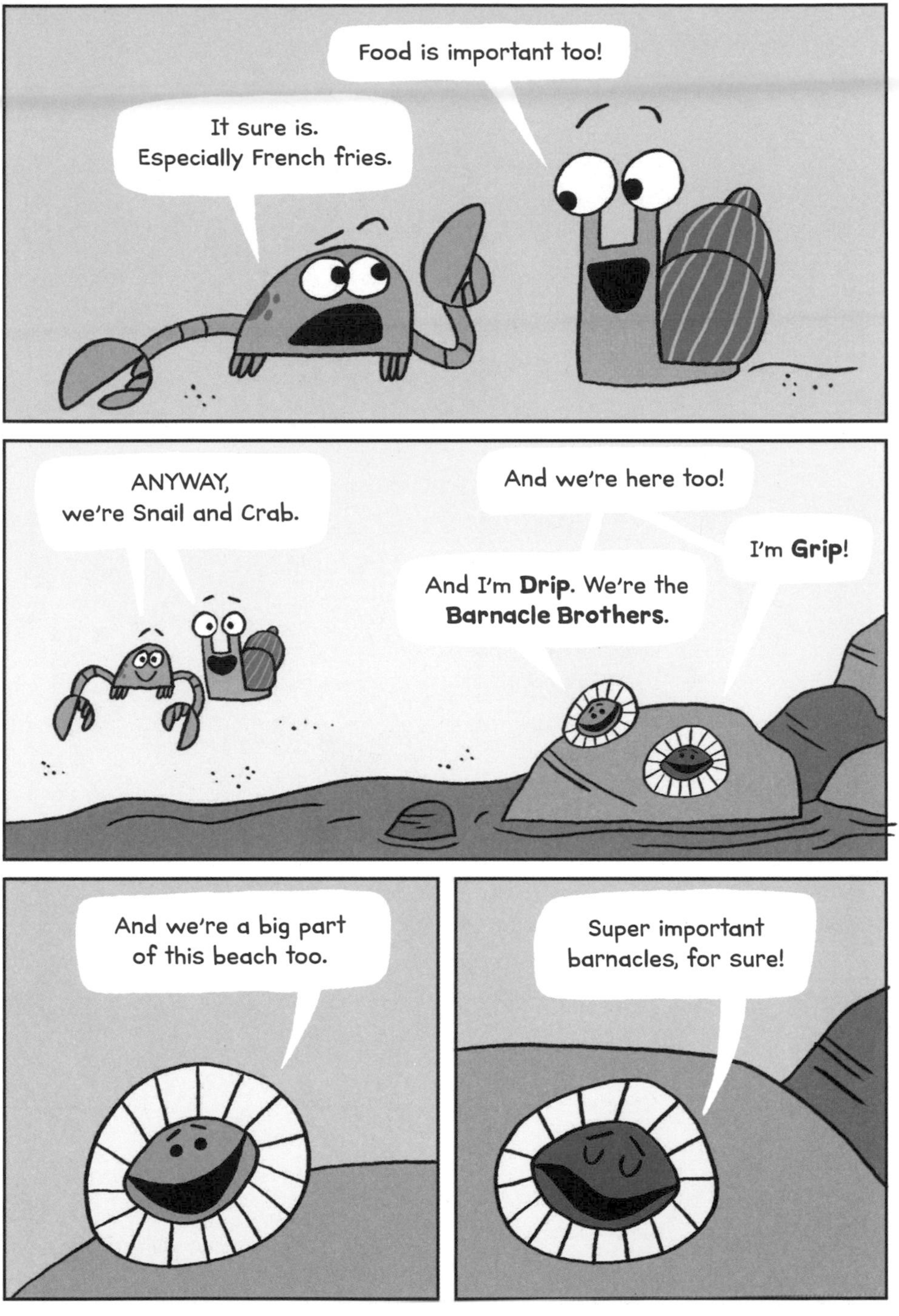
Food is important too!
It sure is. Especially French fries.
ANYWAY, we're Snail and Crab.
And we're here too!
I'm **Grip**!
And I'm **Drip**. We're the **Barnacle Brothers**.
And we're a big part of this beach too.
Super important barnacles, for sure!

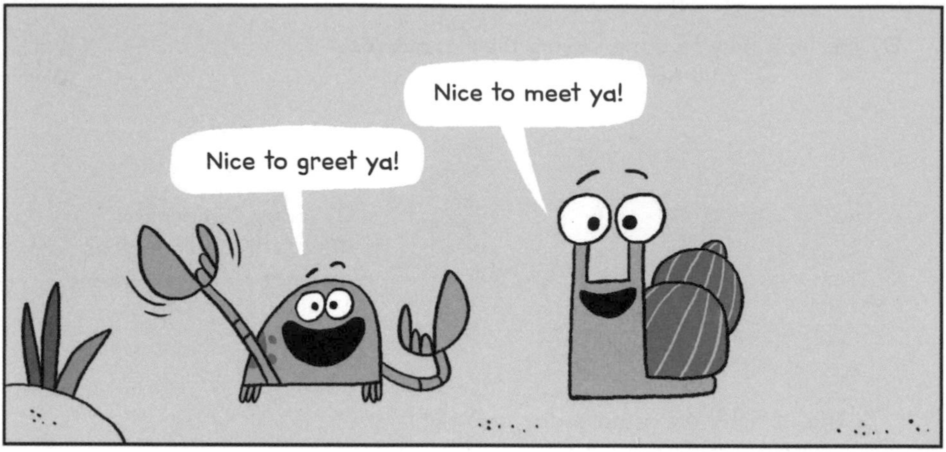
Nice to greet ya!
Nice to meet ya!

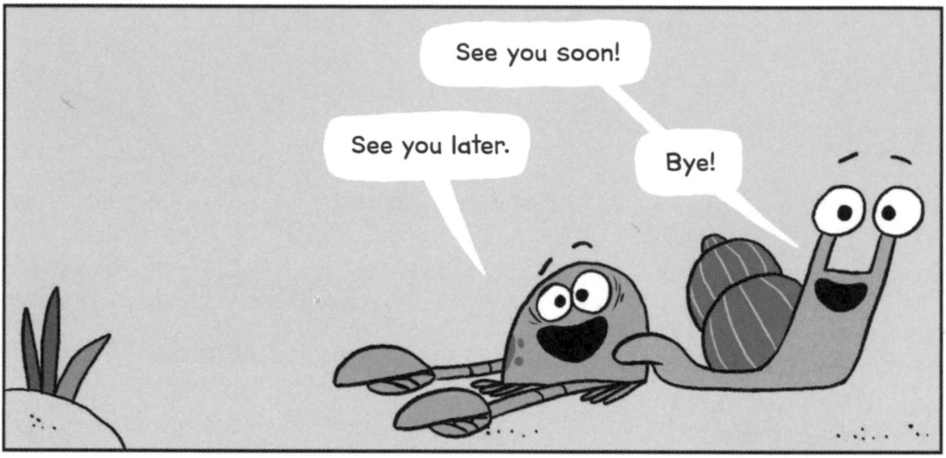
See you soon!
See you later.
Bye!

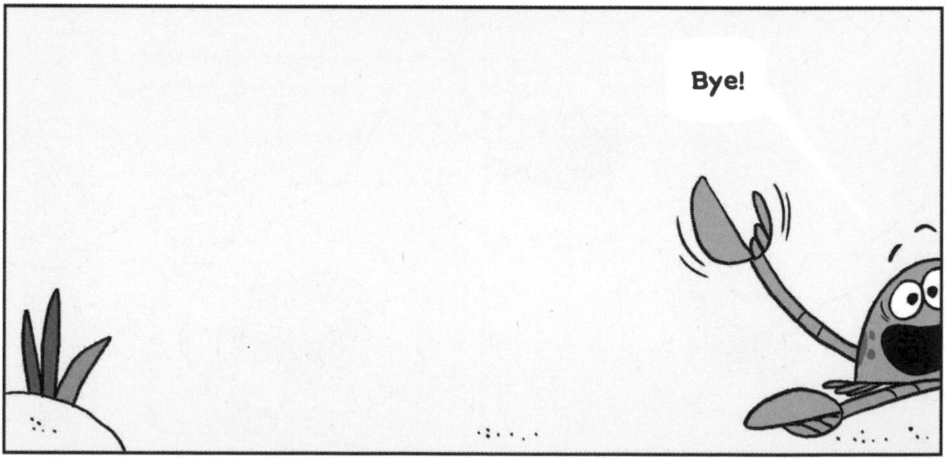
Bye!

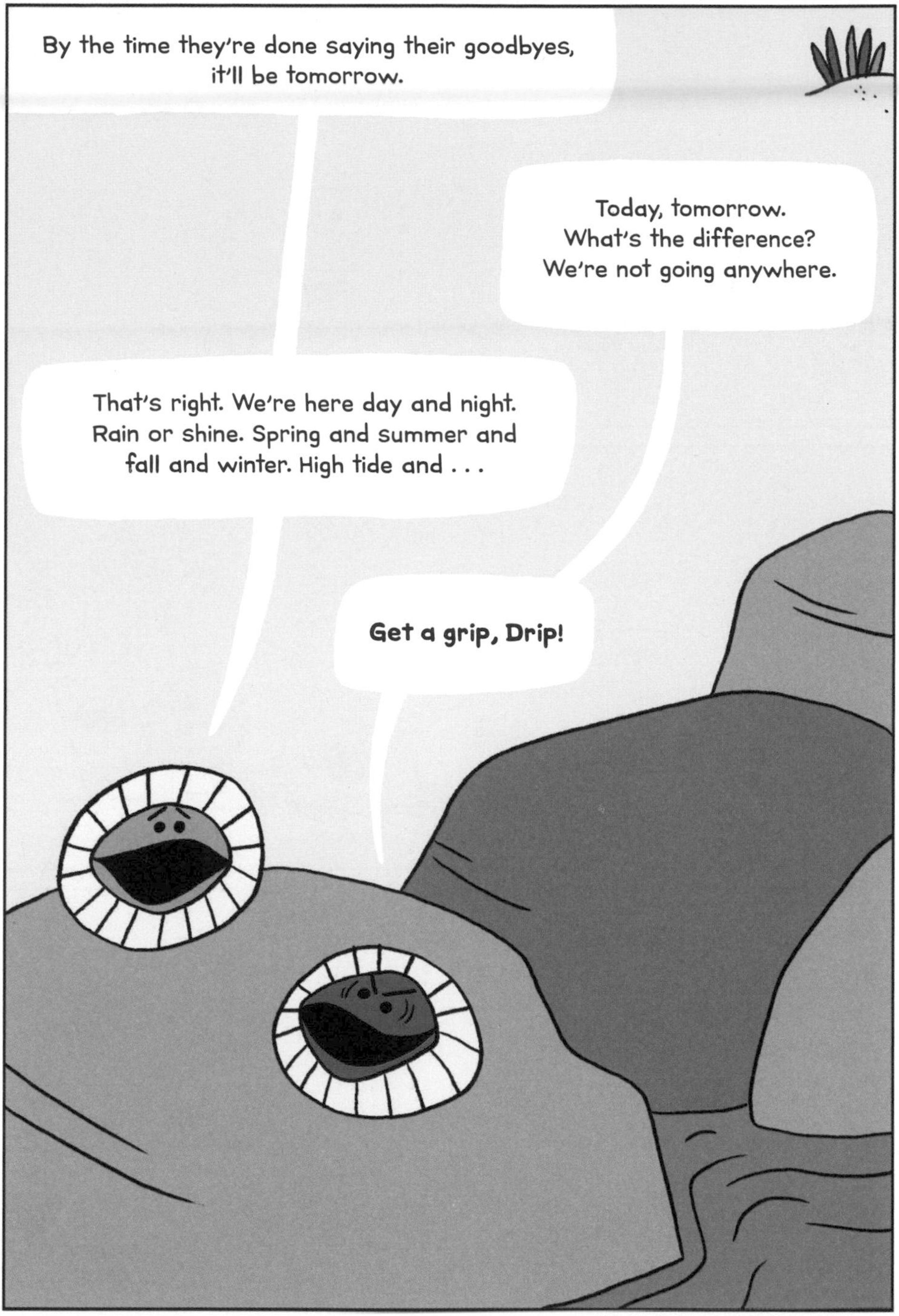

By the time they're done saying their goodbyes, it'll be tomorrow.
Today, tomorrow. What's the difference? We're not going anywhere.
That's right. We're here day and night. Rain or shine. Spring and summer and fall and winter. High tide and . . .
Get a grip, Drip!

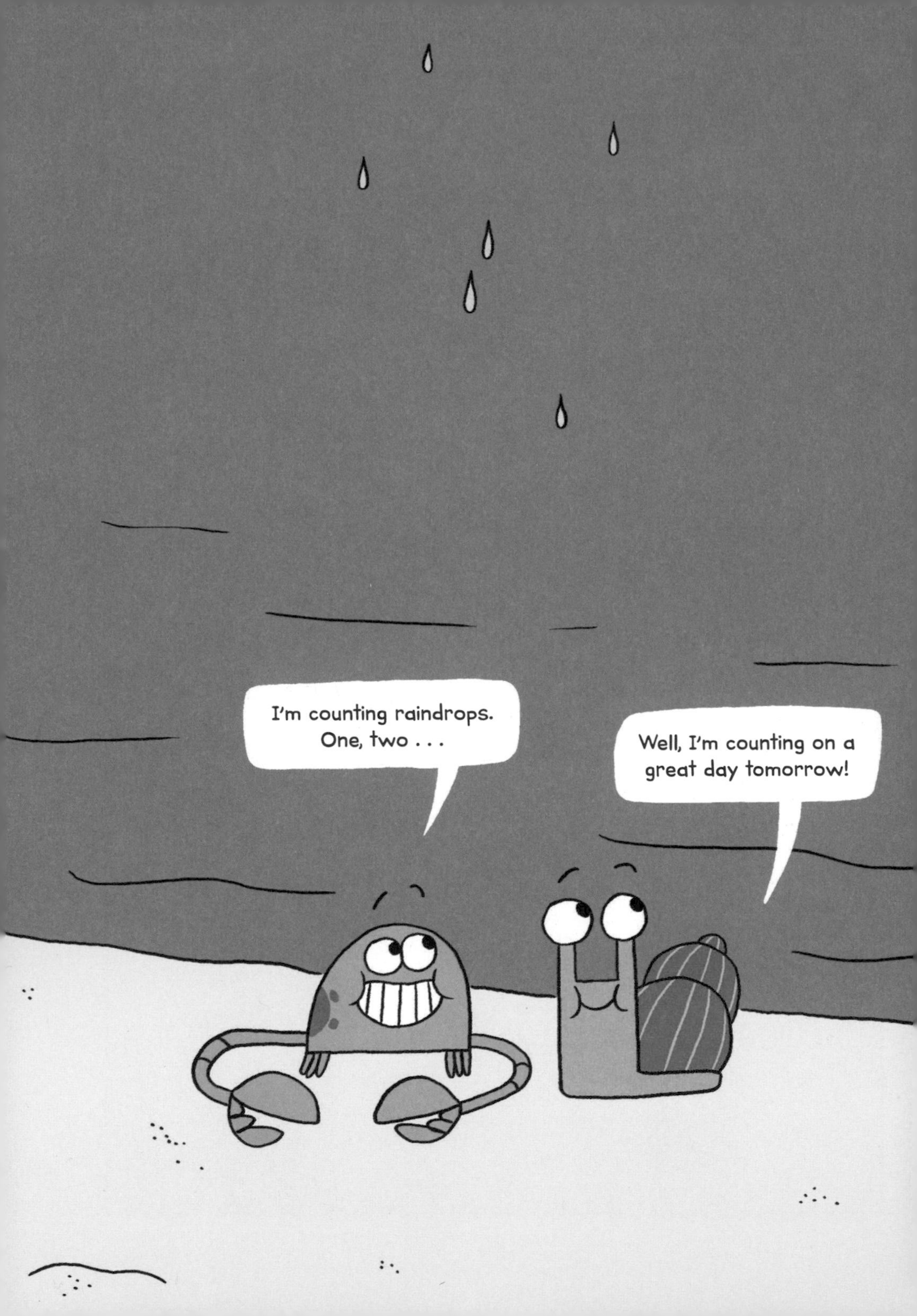
I'm counting raindrops. One, two . . .
Well, I'm counting on a great day tomorrow!

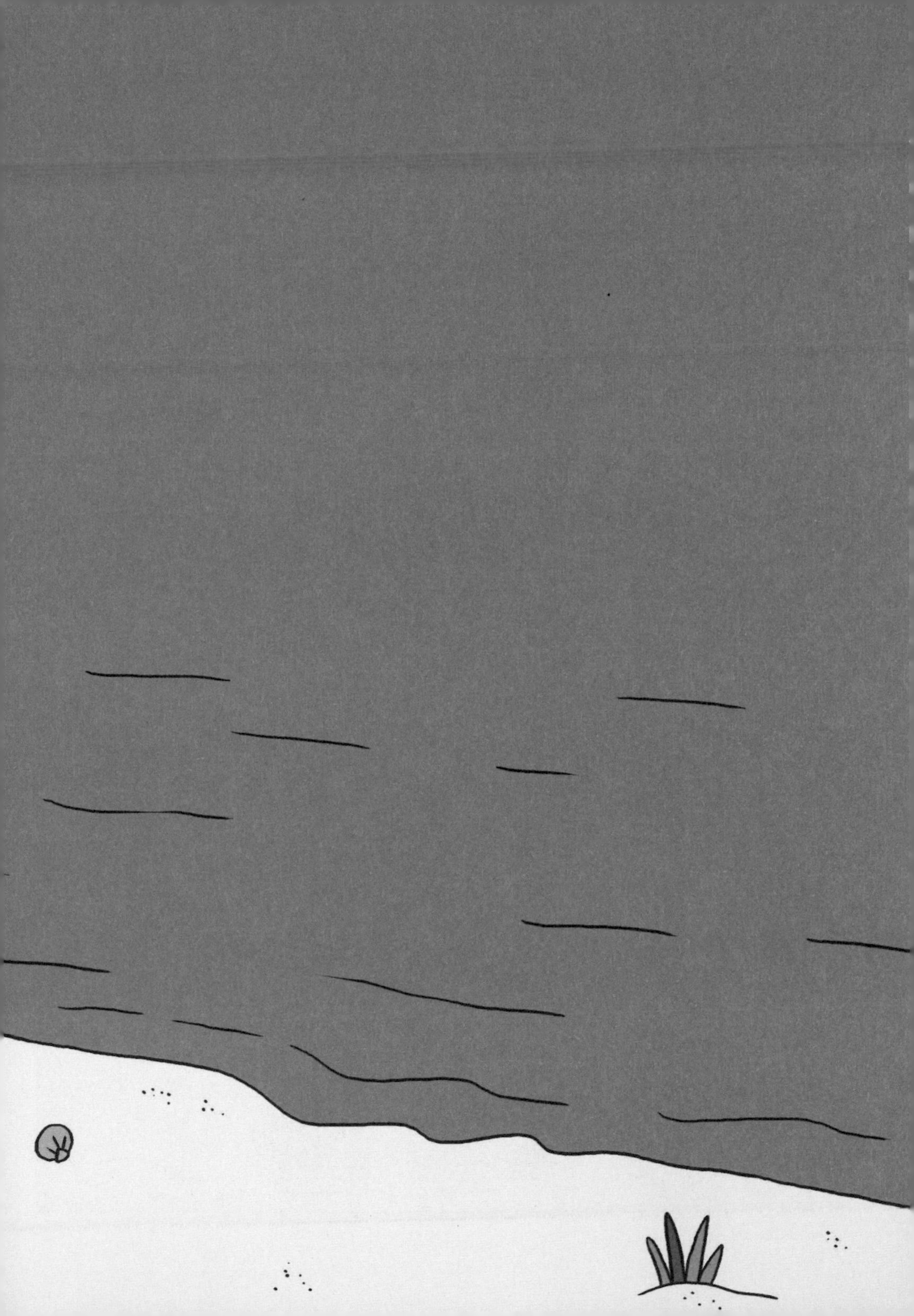

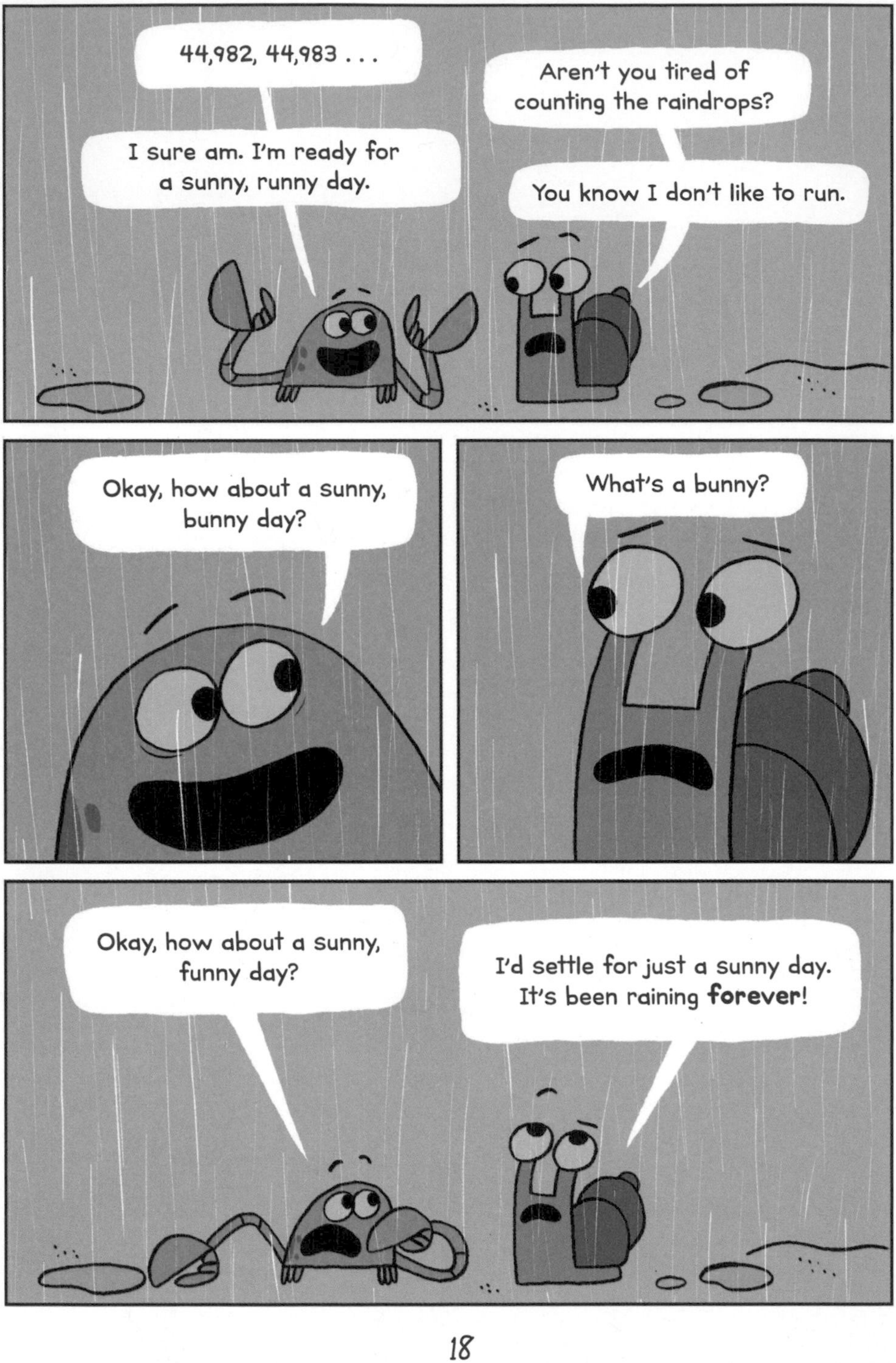
44,982, 44,983 . . .
Aren't you tired of counting the raindrops?
I sure am. I'm ready for a sunny, runny day.
You know I don't like to run.
Okay, how about a sunny, bunny day?
What's a bunny?
Okay, how about a sunny, funny day?
I'd settle for just a sunny day. It's been raining **forever**!

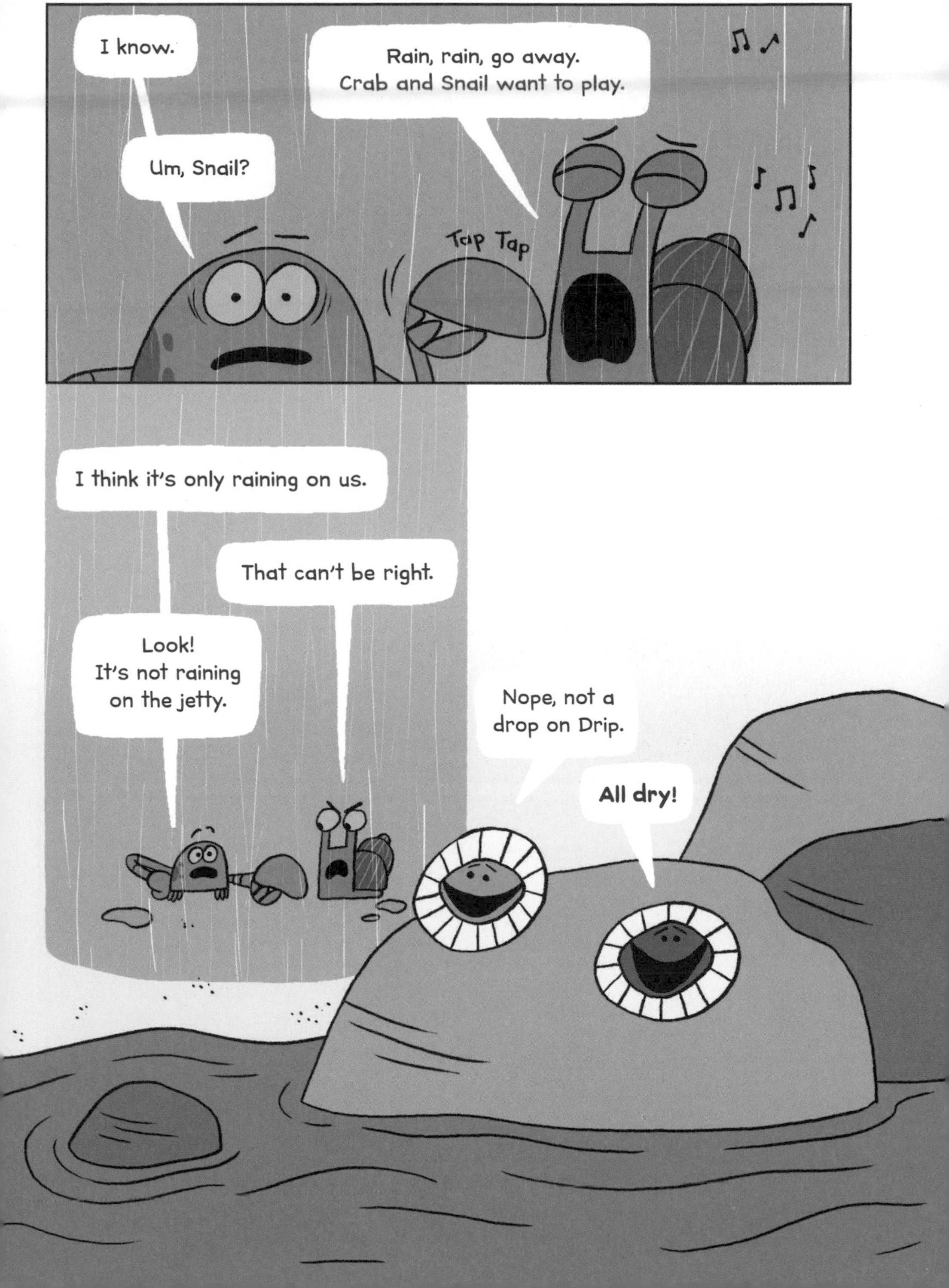

Rain, rain, go away. Crab and Snail want to play.
Um, Snail?
I know.
Tap Tap
I think it's only raining on us.
That can't be right.
Look! It's not raining on the jetty.
Nope, not a drop on Drip.
All dry!

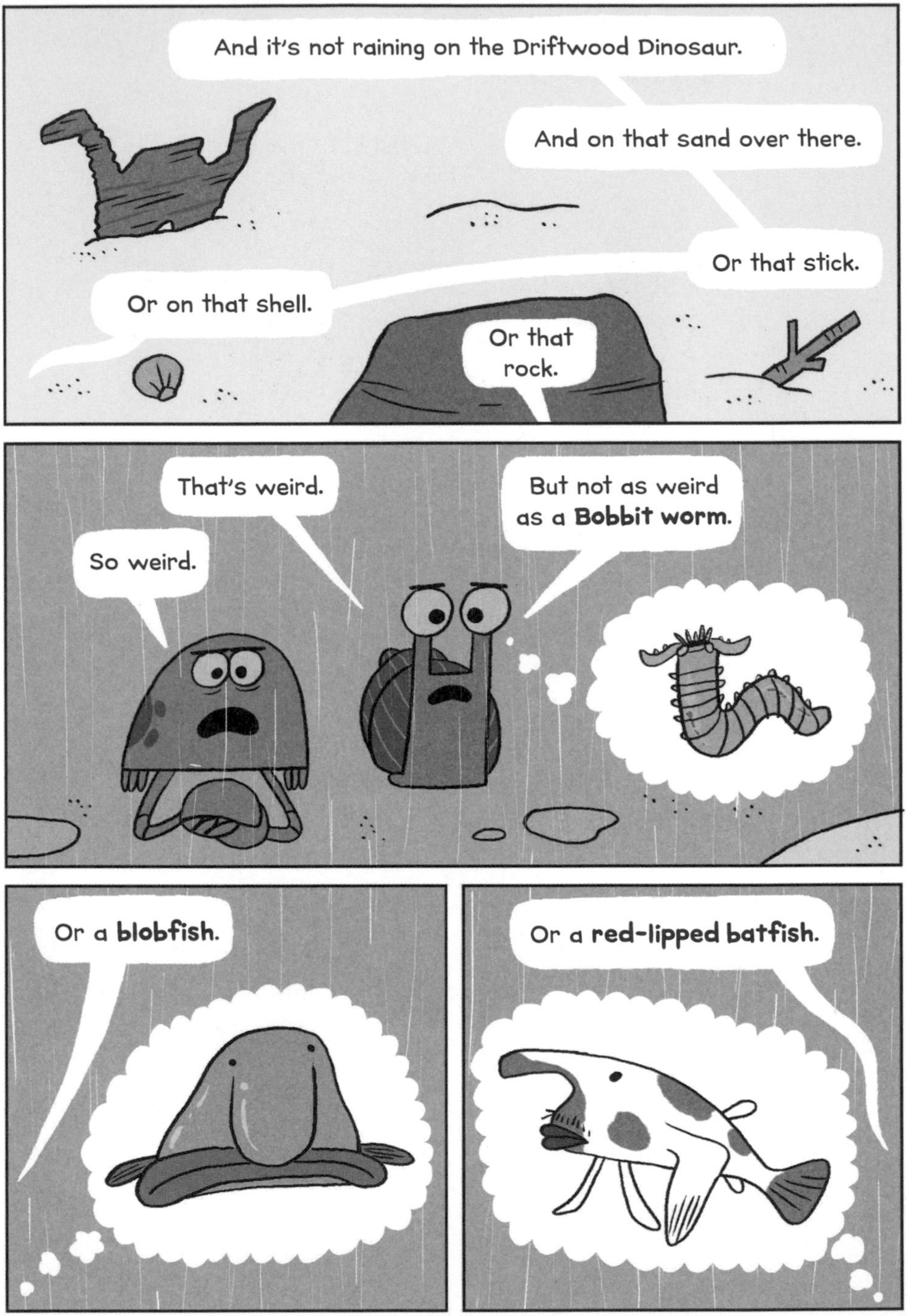
And it's not raining on the Driftwood Dinosaur.
And on that sand over there.
Or that stick.
Or that rock.
Or on that shell.
That's weird.
So weird.
But not as weird as a **Bobbit worm**.
Or a **blobfish**.
Or a **red-lipped batfish**.

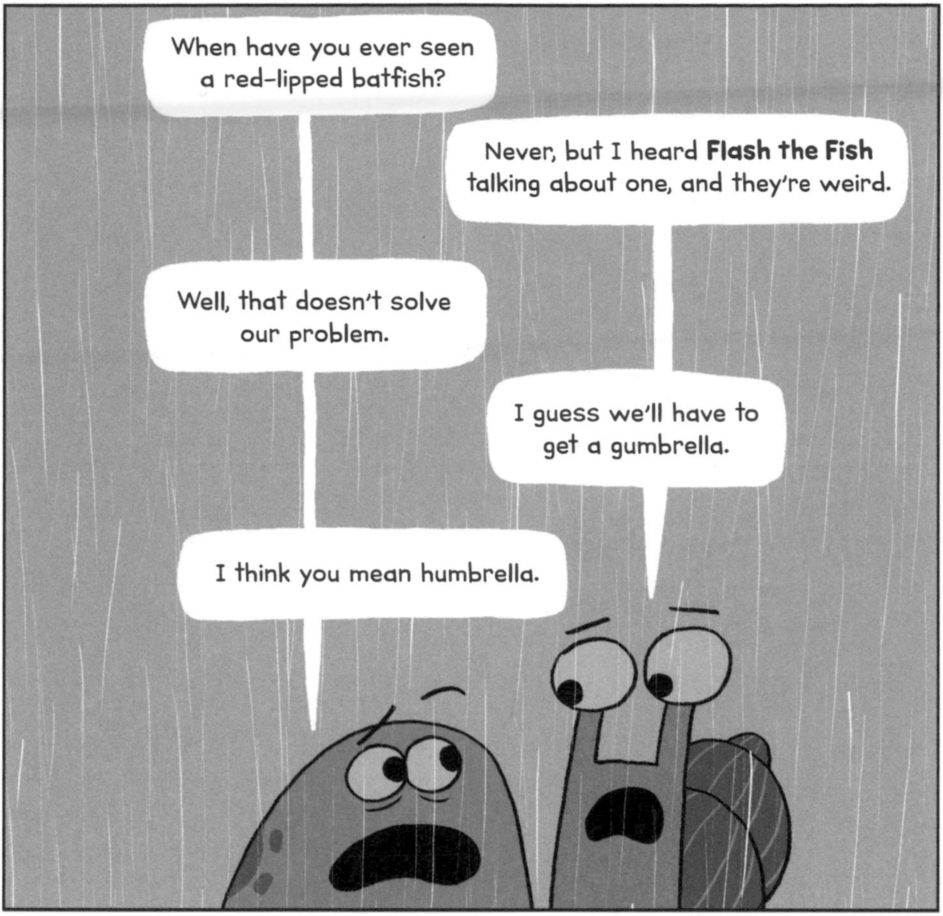
When have you ever seen a red-lipped batfish?
Never, but I heard **Flash the Fish** talking about one, and they're weird.
Well, that doesn't solve our problem.
I guess we'll have to get a gumbrella.
I think you mean humbrella.

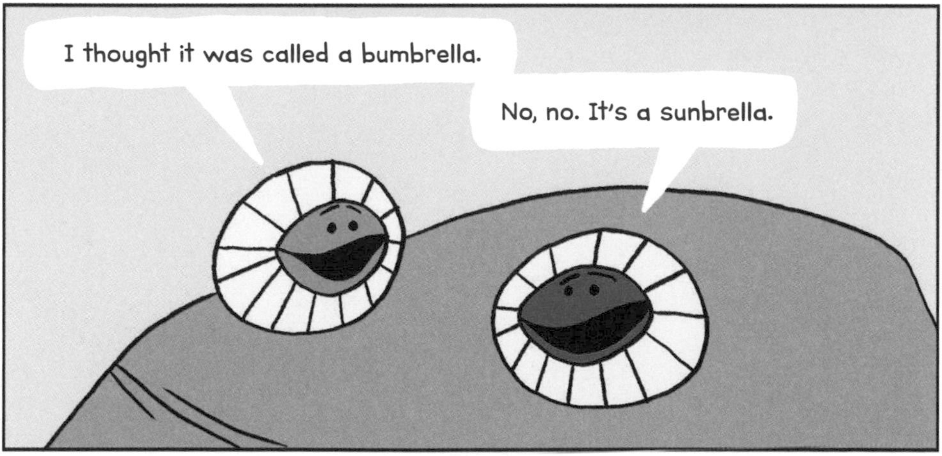
I thought it was called a bumbrella.
No, no. It's a sunbrella.

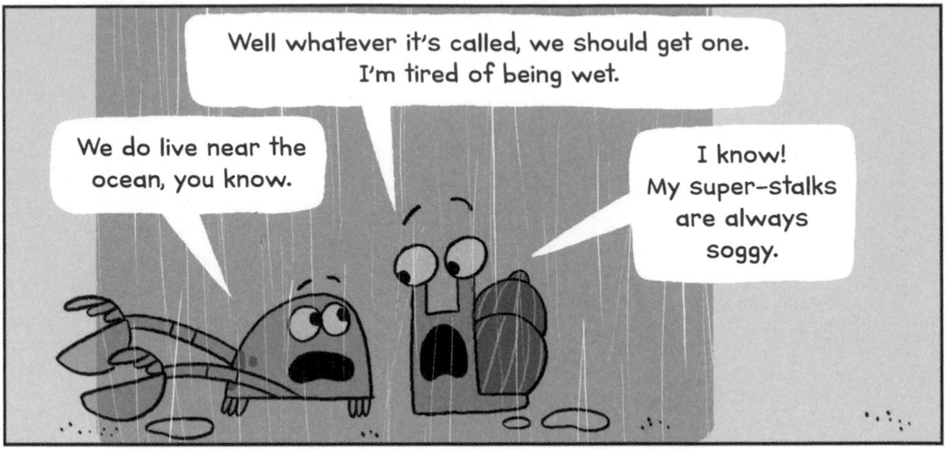
We do live near the ocean, you know.
Well whatever it's called, we should get one. I'm tired of being wet.
I know! My super-stalks are always soggy.

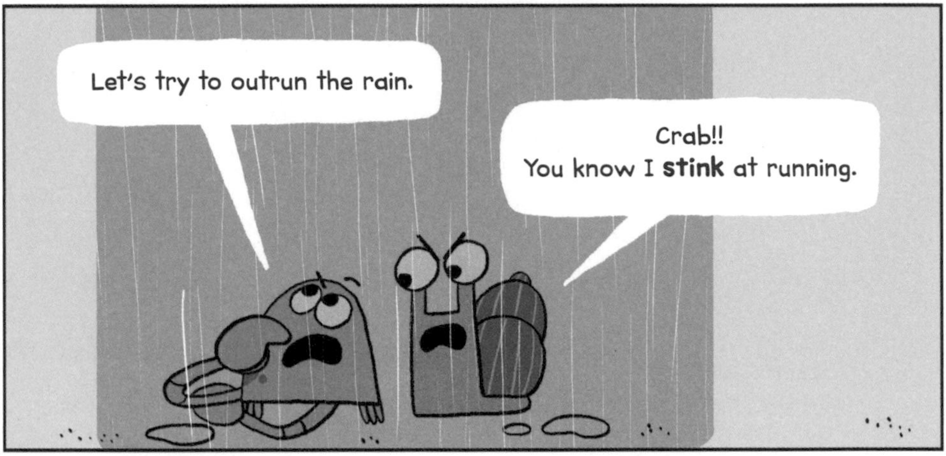
Let's try to outrun the rain.
Crab!! You know I **stink** at running.

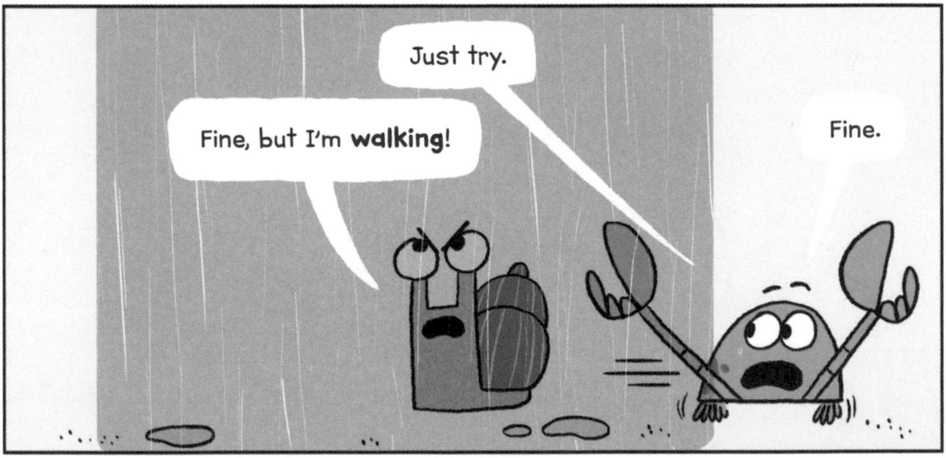
Just try.
Fine, but I'm **walking**!
Fine.

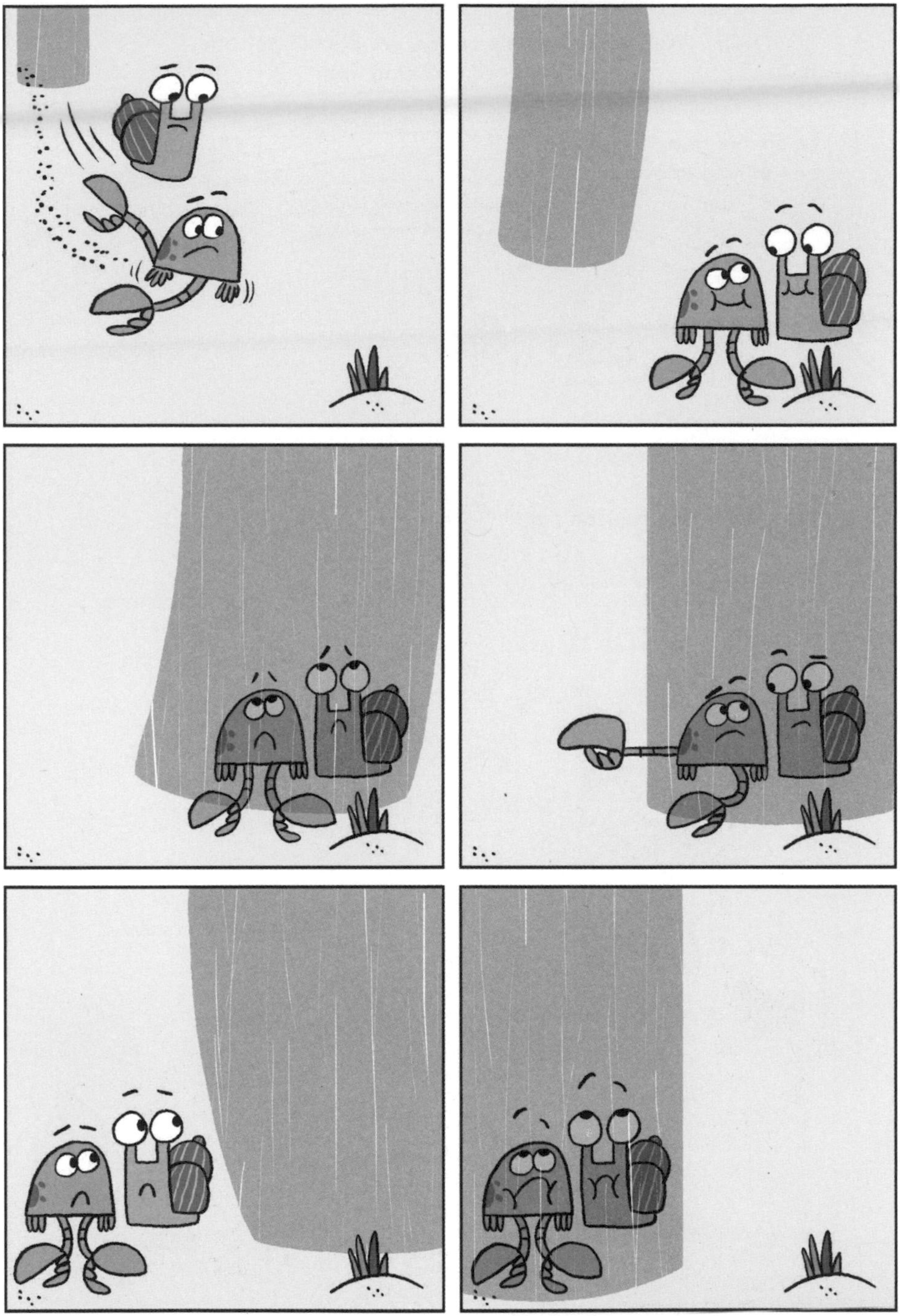

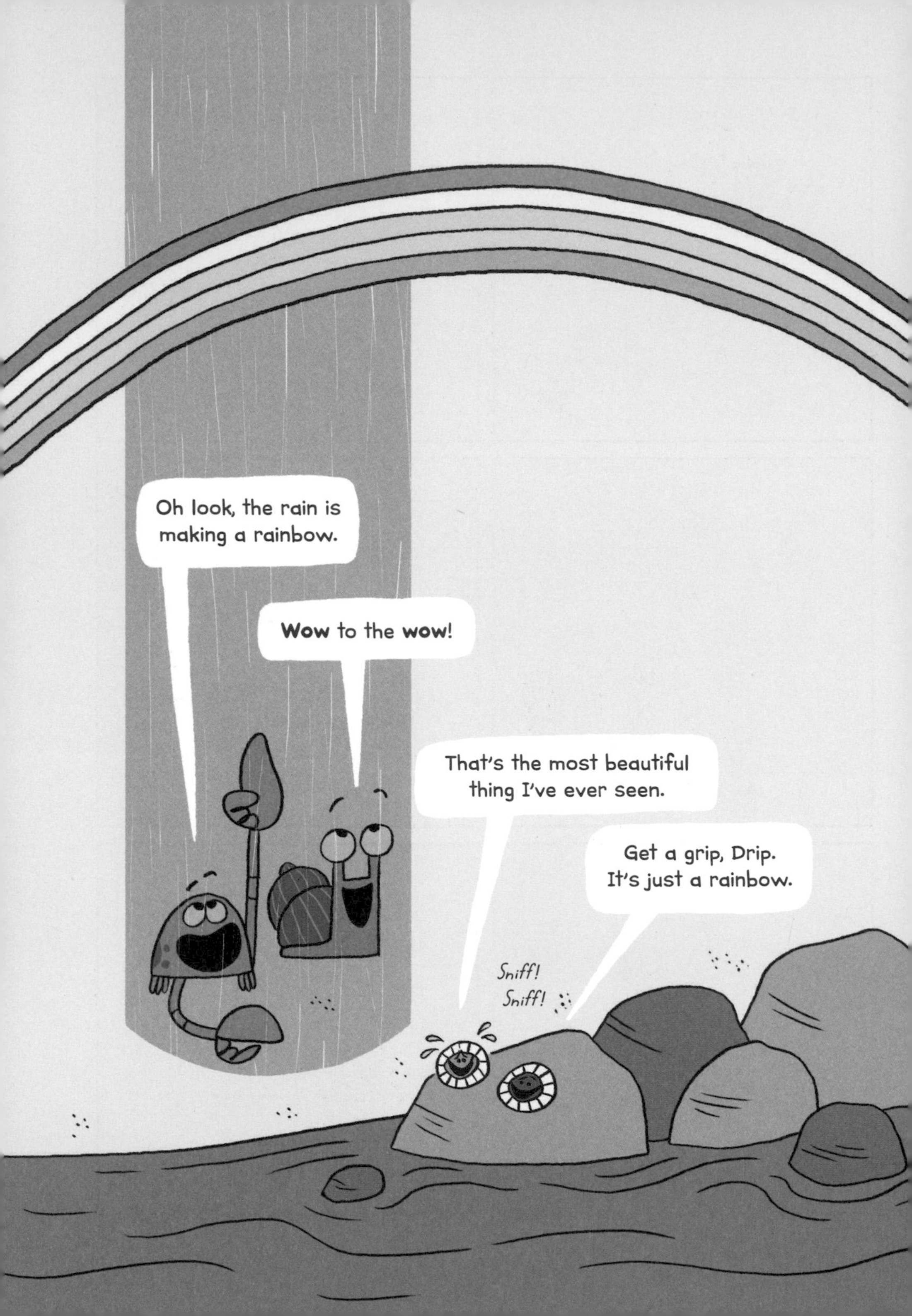
Oh look, the rain is making a rainbow.
Wow to the **wow**!
That's the most beautiful thing I've ever seen.
Sniff! Sniff!
Get a grip, Drip. It's just a rainbow.

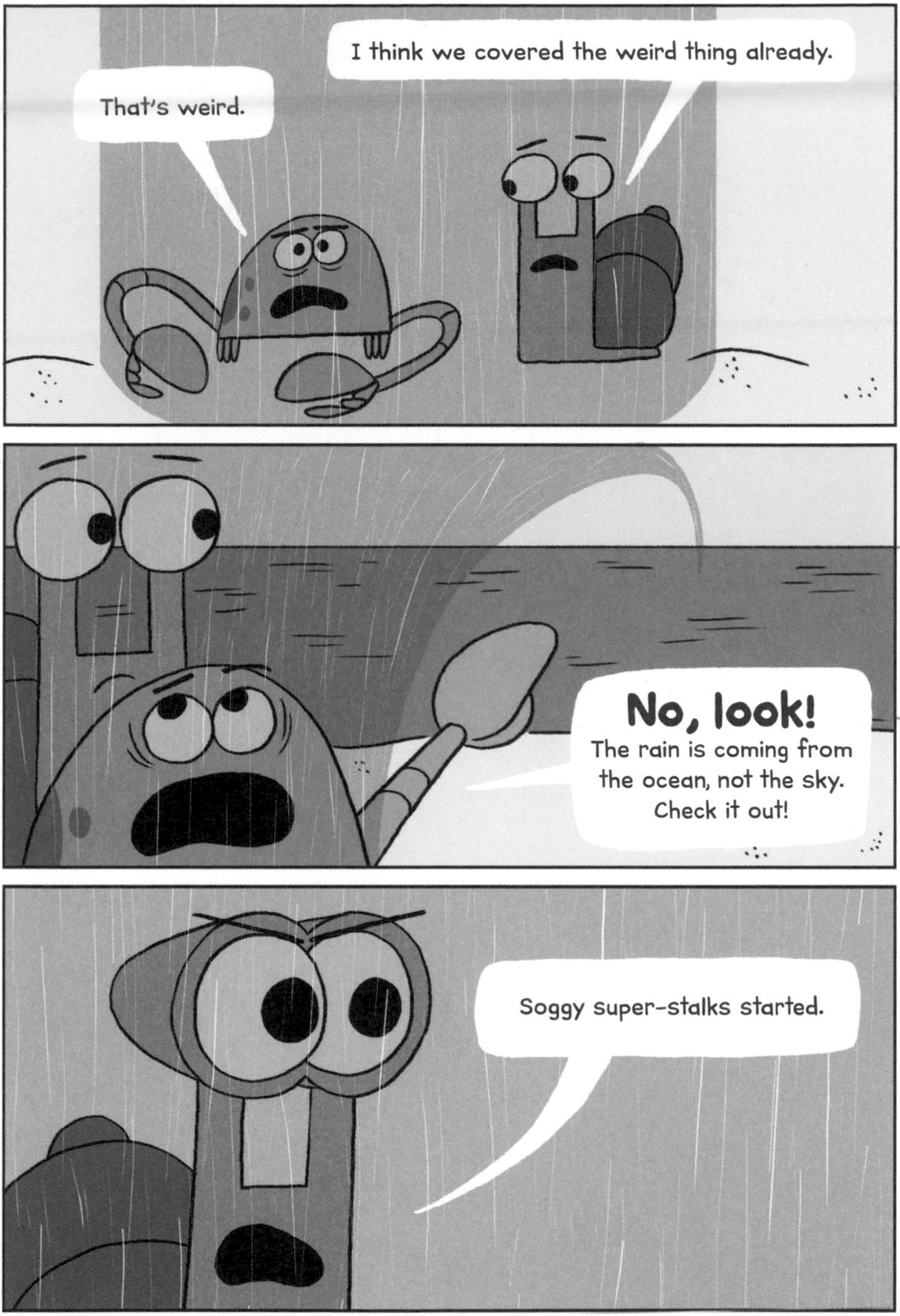
That's weird.
I think we covered the weird thing already.
No, look!
The rain is coming from the ocean, not the sky. Check it out!
Soggy super-stalks started.

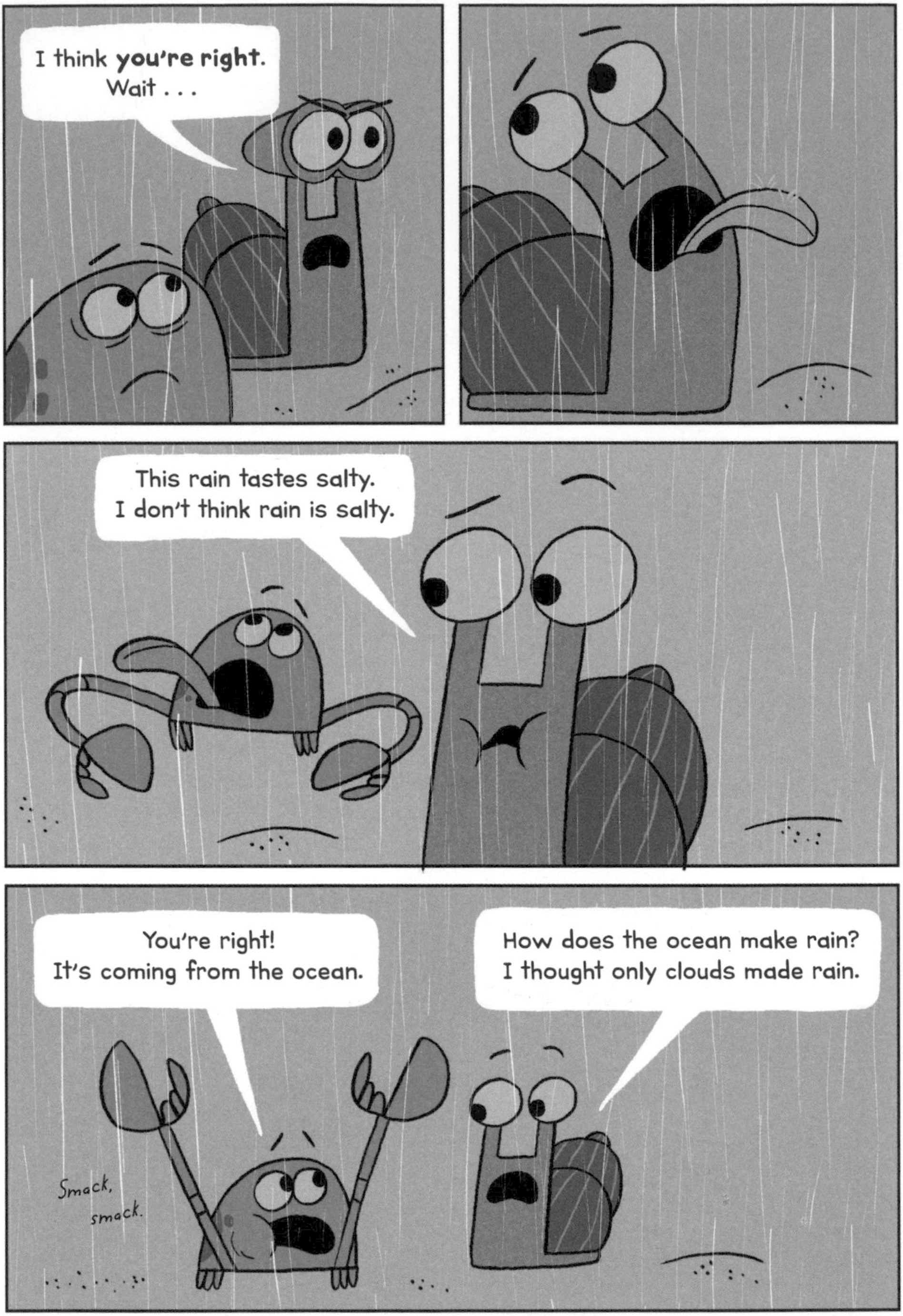
I think **you're right**.
Wait . . .
This rain tastes salty.
I don't think rain is salty.
You're right!
It's coming from the ocean.
How does the ocean make rain?
I thought only clouds made rain.
Smack,
smack.

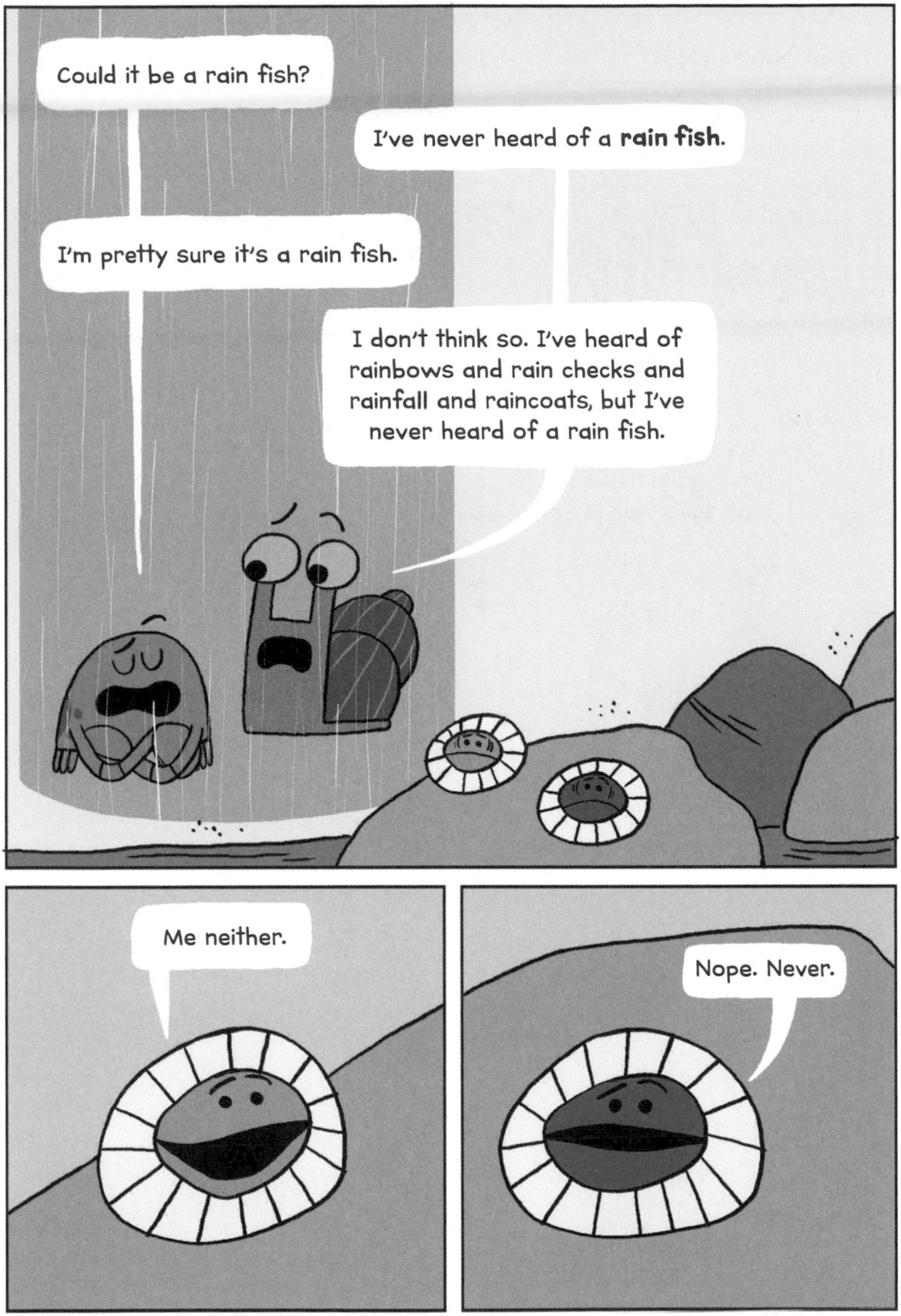
Could it be a rain fish?
I've never heard of a **rain fish**.
I'm pretty sure it's a rain fish.
I don't think so. I've heard of rainbows and rain checks and rainfall and raincoats, but I've never heard of a rain fish.
Me neither.
Nope. Never.

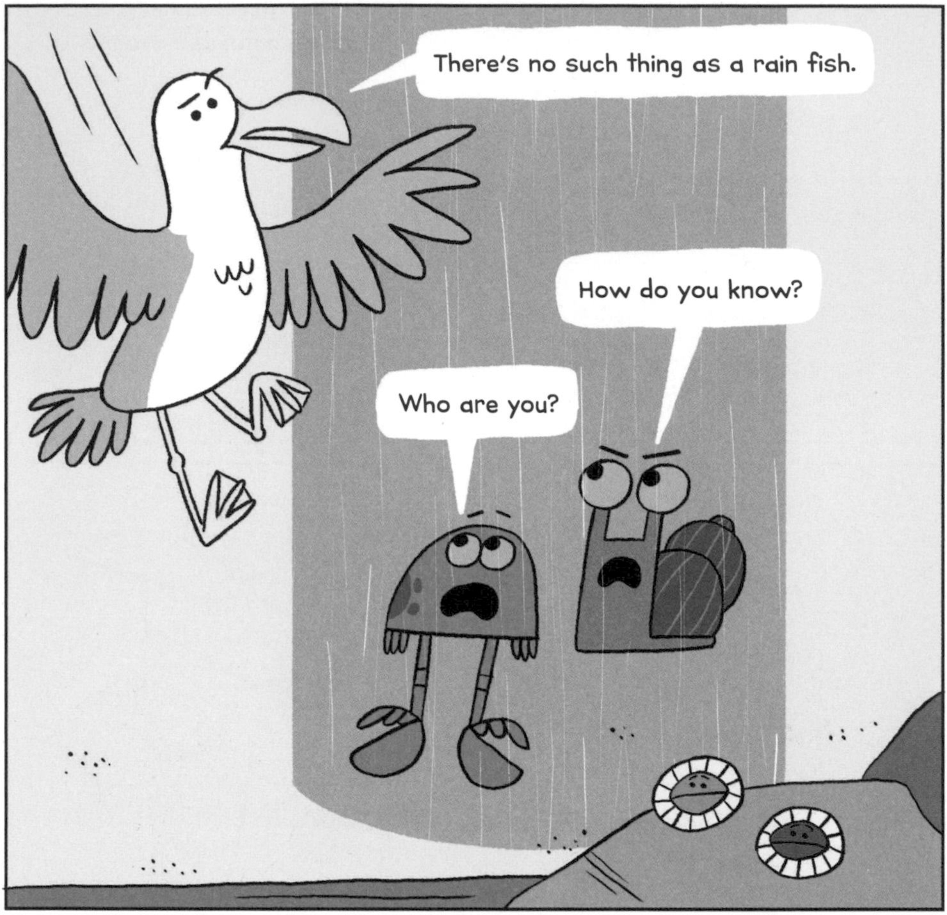
There's no such thing as a rain fish.
Who are you?
How do you know?

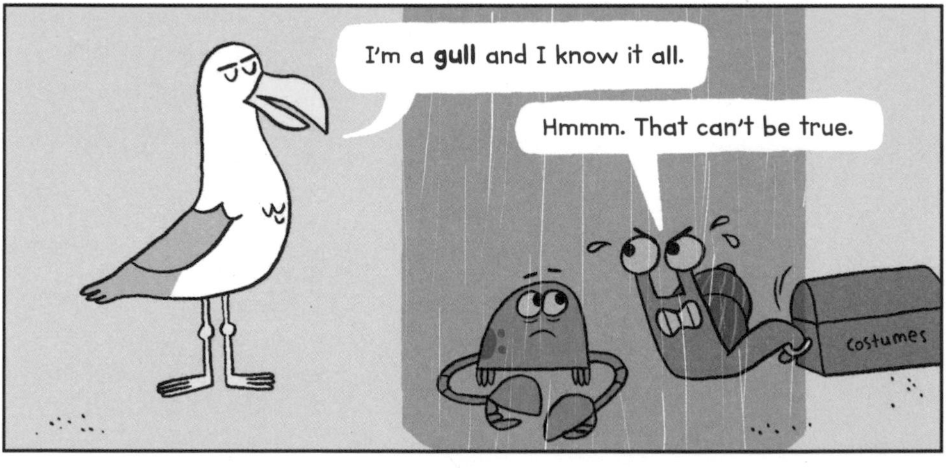
I'm a **gull** and I know it all.
Hmmm. That can't be true.
COSTUMES

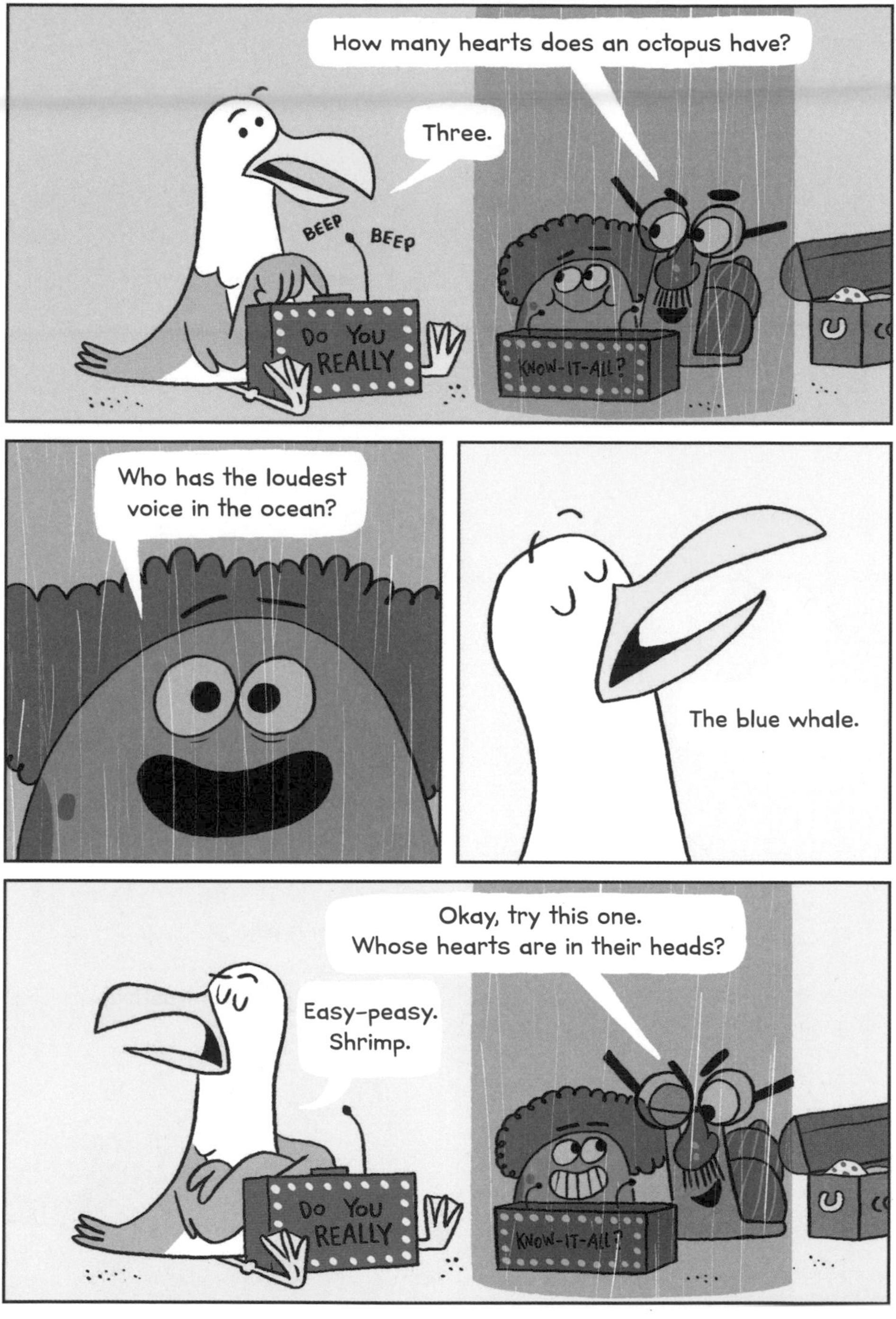
How many hearts does an octopus have?
Three.
BEEP BEEP
DO YOU REALLY
KNOW-IT-ALL?
Who has the loudest voice in the ocean?
The blue whale.
Okay, try this one. Whose hearts are in their heads?
Easy-peasy. Shrimp.
DO YOU REALLY
KNOW-IT-ALL?

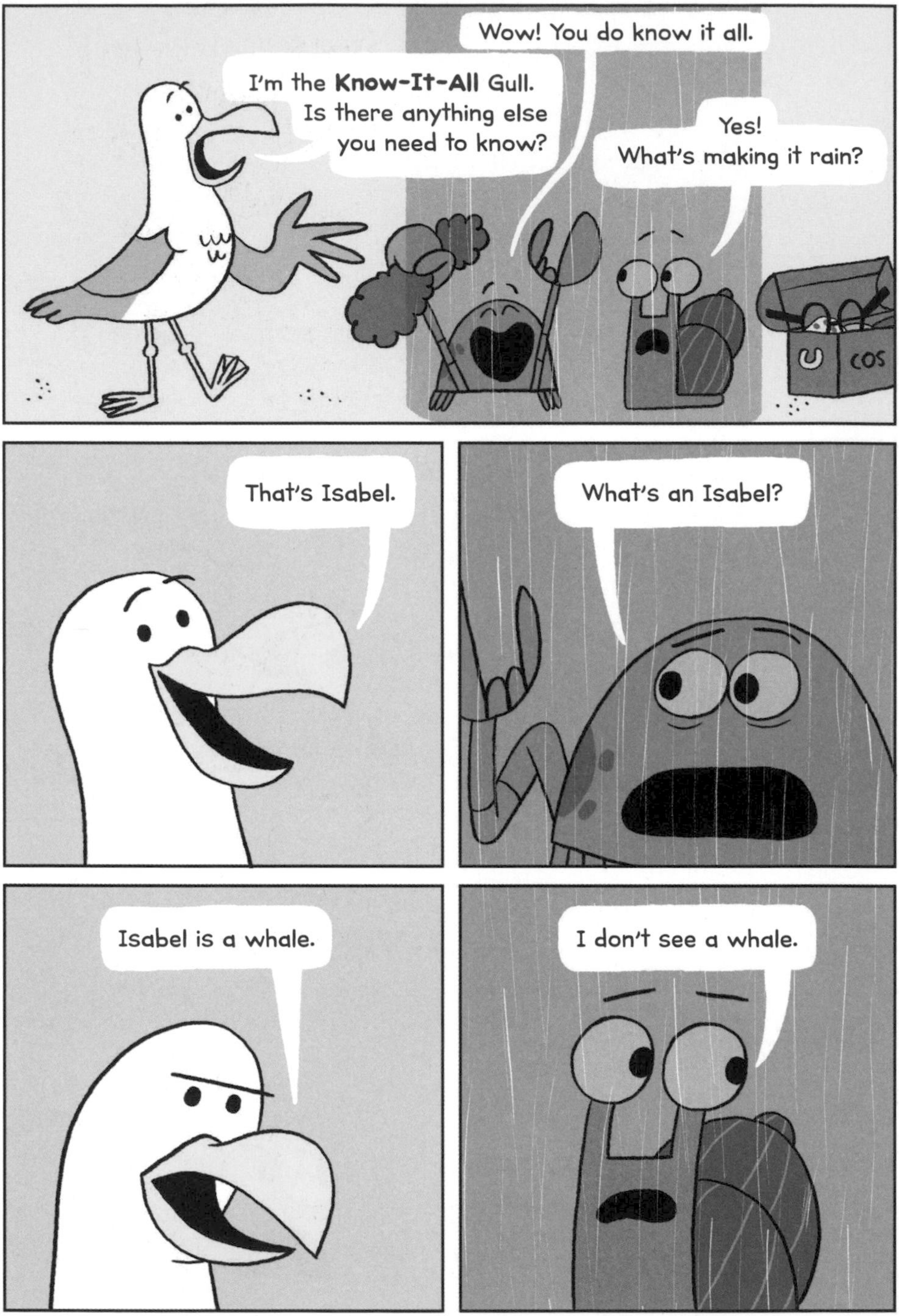

I'm the **Know-It-All** Gull. Is there anything else you need to know?
Wow! You do know it all.
Yes! What's making it rain?
COS
That's Isabel.
What's an Isabel?
Isabel is a whale.
I don't see a whale.

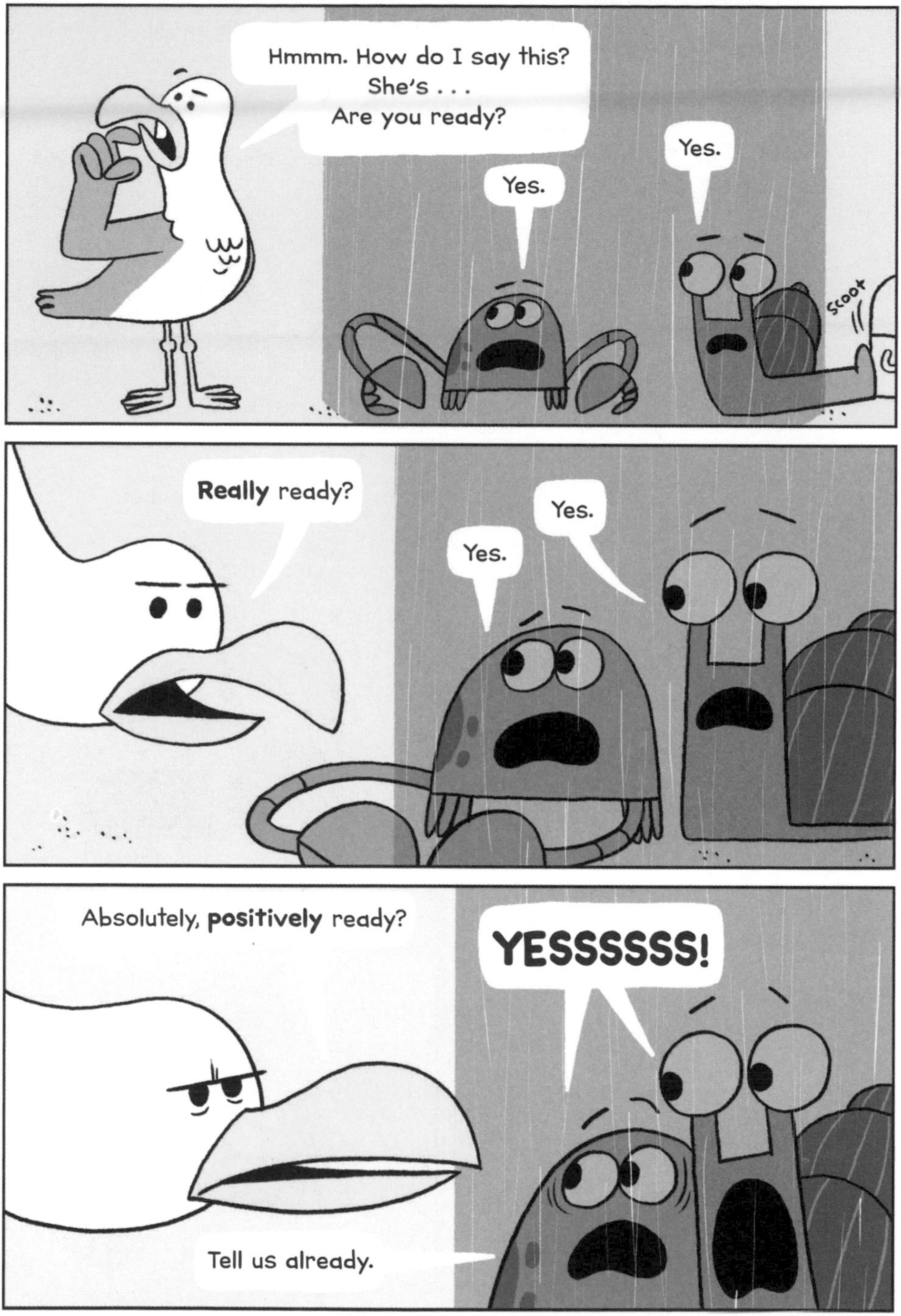
Hmmm. How do I say this? She's . . . Are you ready?
Yes.
Yes.
scoot
Really ready?
Yes.
Yes.
Absolutely, **positively** ready?
YESSSSSS!
Tell us already.

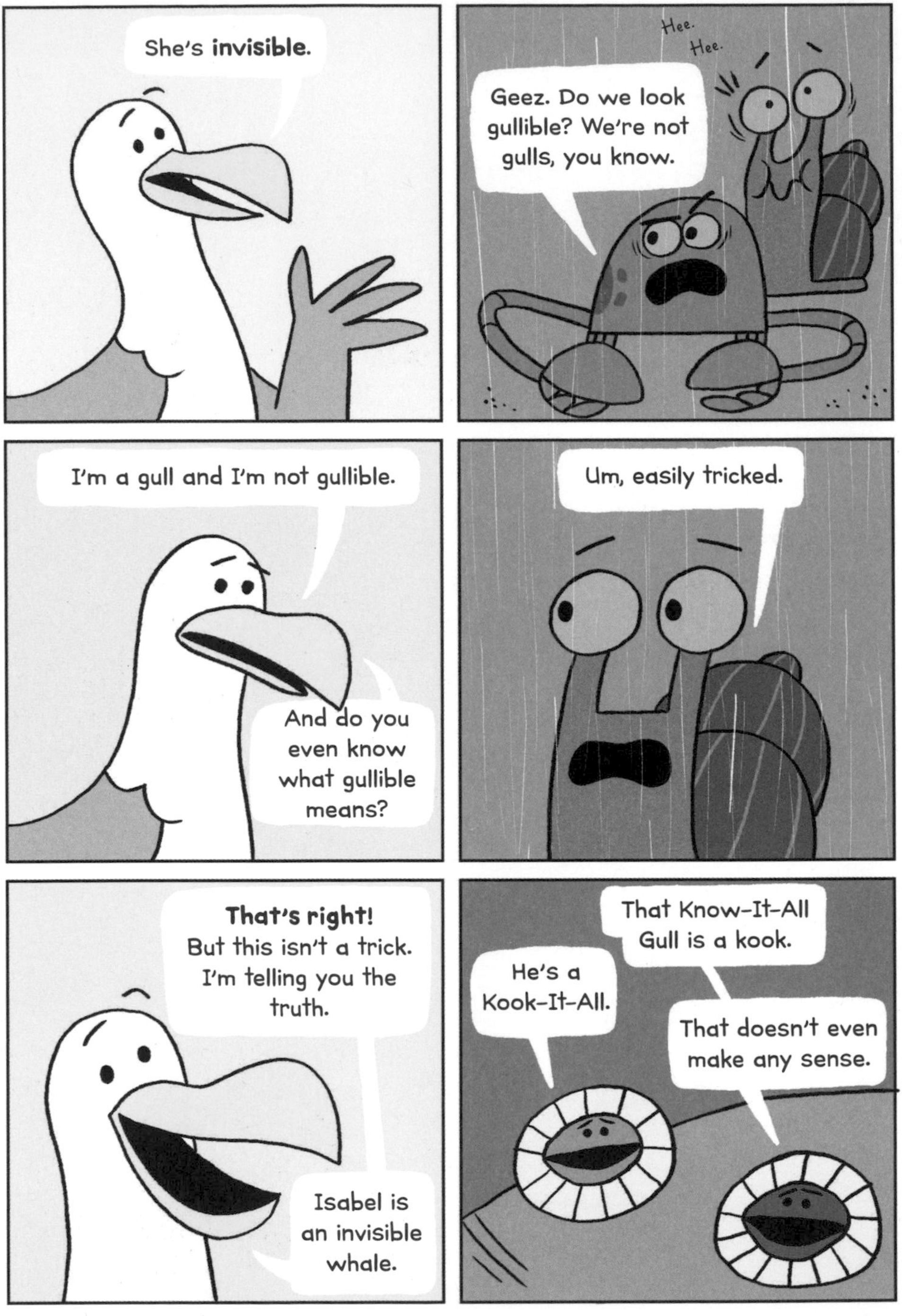
She's **invisible.**
Hee. Hee.
Geez. Do we look gullible? We're not gulls, you know.
I'm a gull and I'm not gullible.
And do you even know what gullible means?
Um, easily tricked.
That's right! But this isn't a trick. I'm telling you the truth.
Isabel is an invisible whale.
That Know-It-All Gull is a kook.
He's a Kook-It-All.
That doesn't even make any sense.

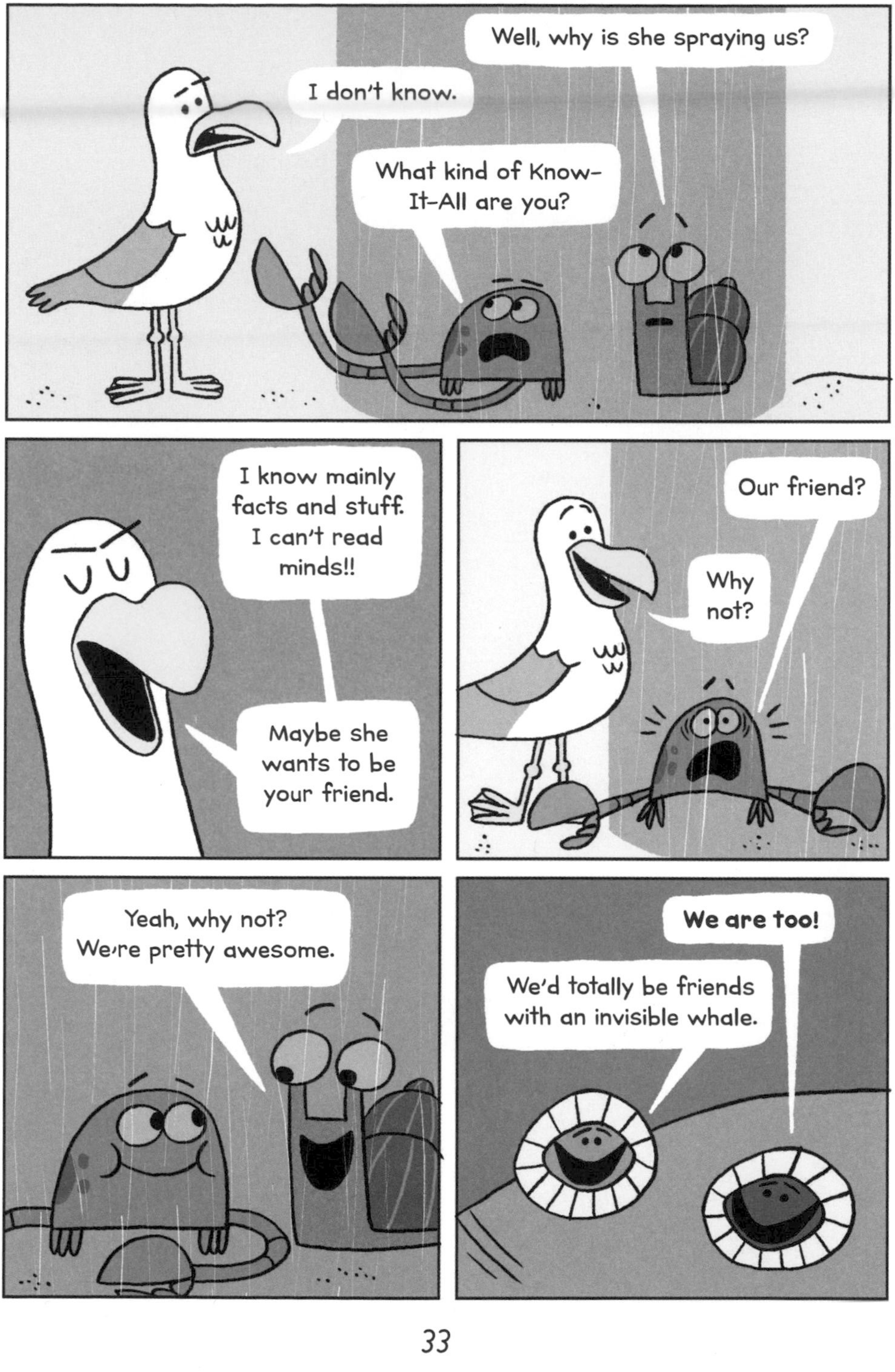

I don't know.
Well, why is she spraying us?
What kind of Know-It-All are you?
I know mainly facts and stuff. I can't read minds!!
Maybe she wants to be your friend.
Why not?
Our friend?
Yeah, why not? We're pretty awesome.
We'd totally be friends with an invisible whale.
We are too!

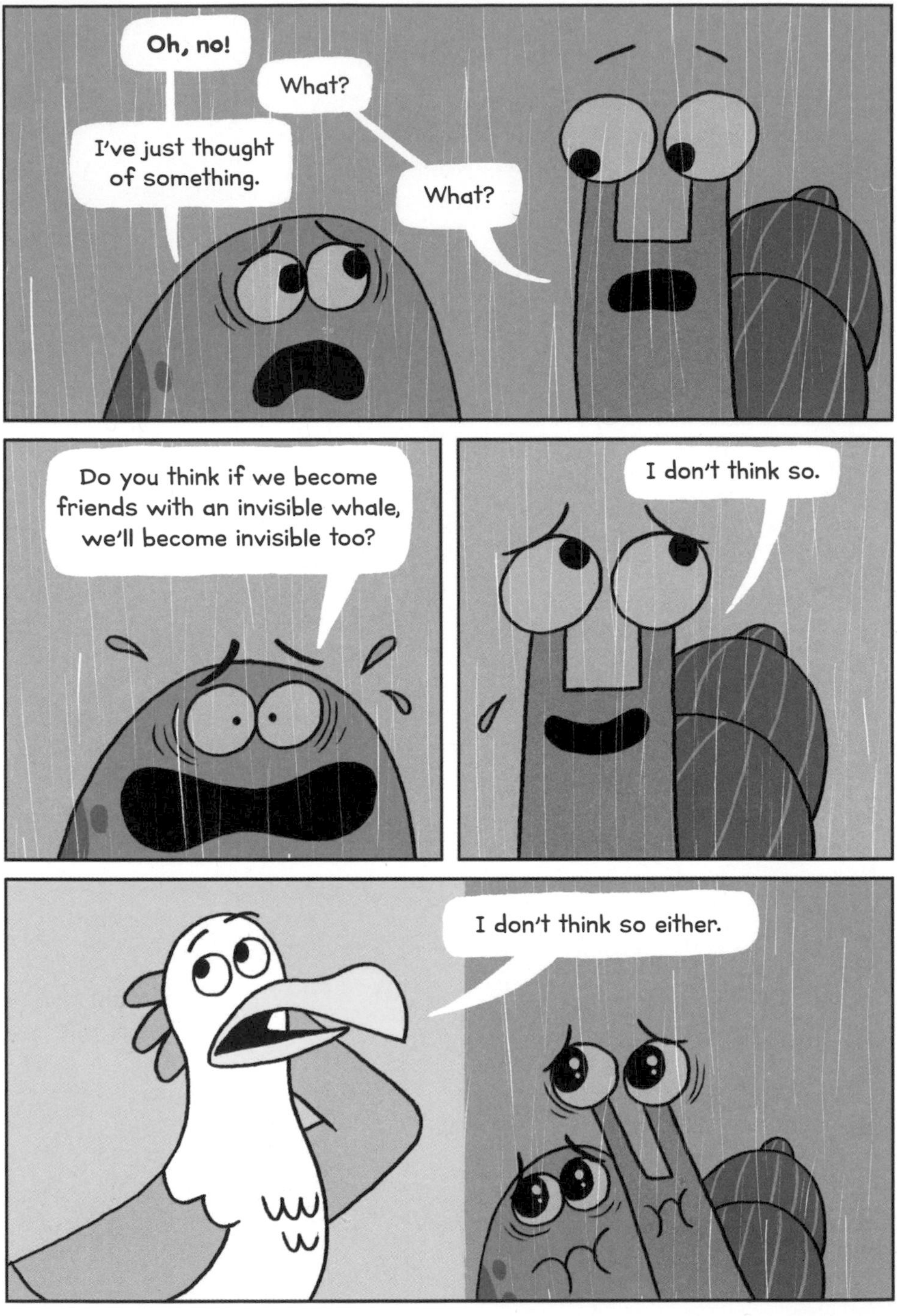

Oh, no!
I've just thought of something.
What?
What?
Do you think if we become friends with an invisible whale, we'll become invisible too?
I don't think so.
I don't think so either.

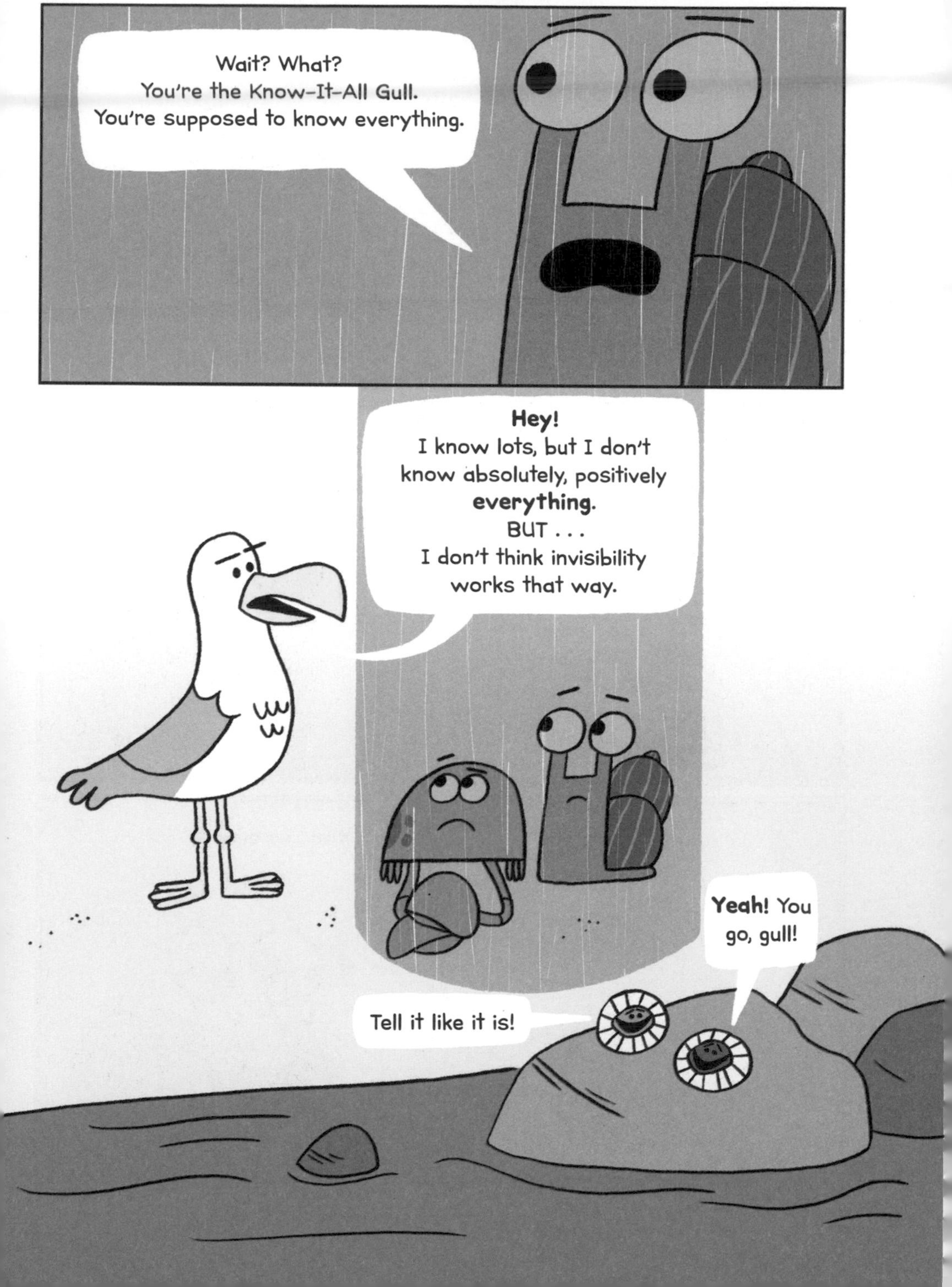

Wait? What? You're the Know-It-All Gull. You're supposed to know everything.
Hey! I know lots, but I don't know absolutely, positively **everything.** BUT . . . I don't think invisibility works that way.
Tell it like it is!
Yeah! You go, gull!

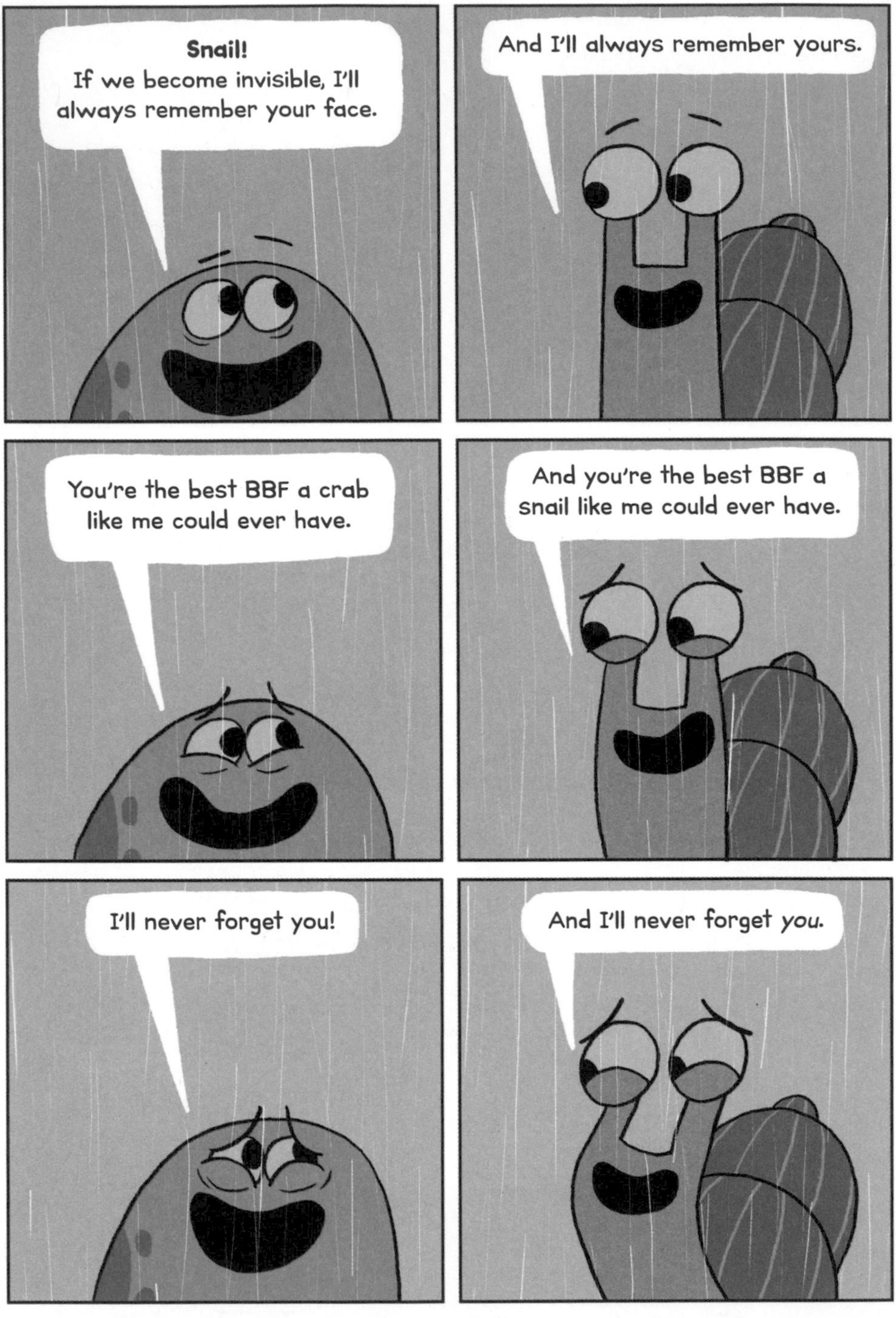
Snail! If we become invisible, I'll always remember your face.
And I'll always remember yours.
You're the best BBF a crab like me could ever have.
And you're the best BBF a snail like me could ever have.
I'll never forget you!
And I'll never forget *you*.

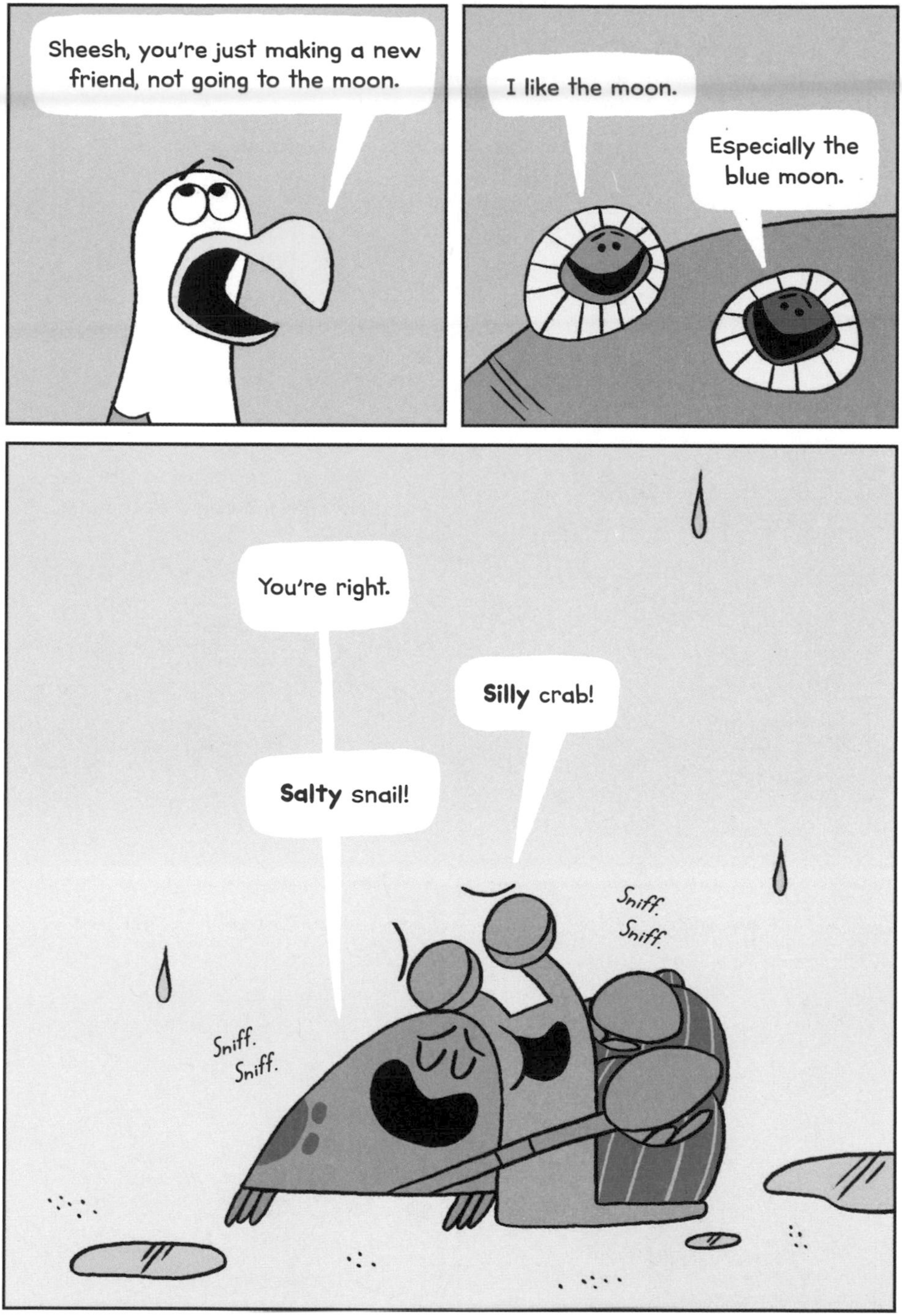
Sheesh, you're just making a new friend, not going to the moon.
I like the moon.
Especially the blue moon.
You're right.
Silly crab!
Salty snail!
Sniff. Sniff.
Sniff. Sniff.

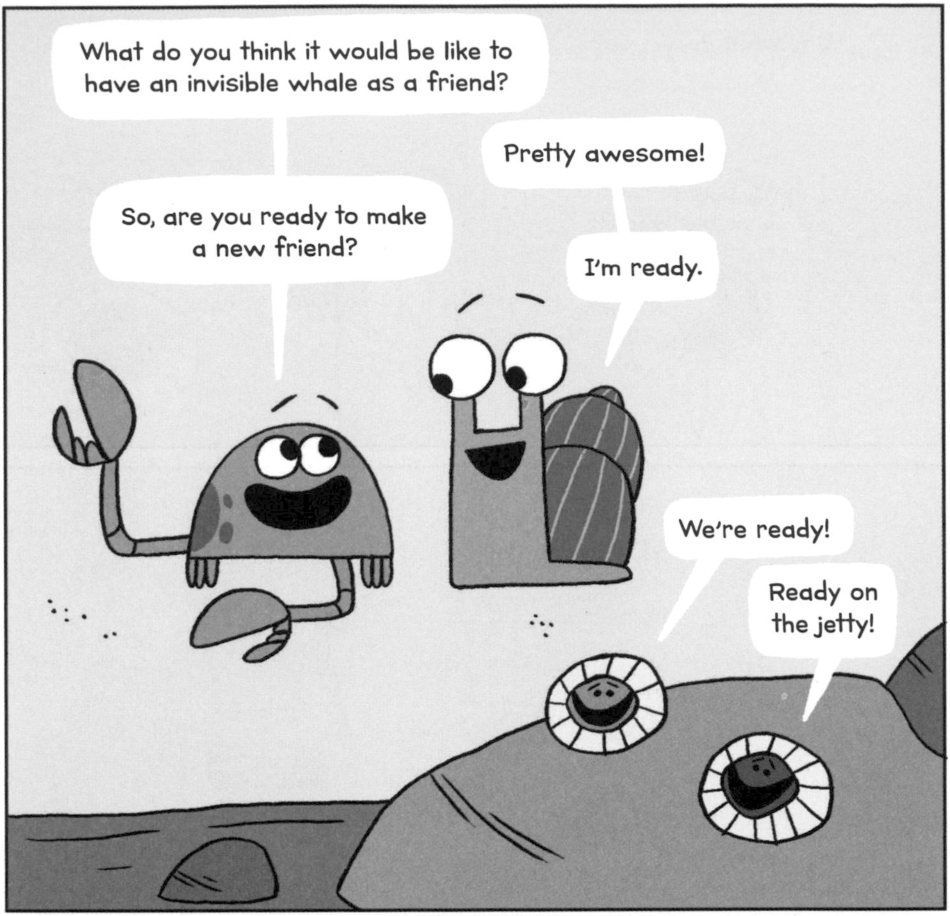
What do you think it would be like to have an invisible whale as a friend?
Pretty awesome!
So, are you ready to make a new friend?
I'm ready.
We're ready!
Ready on the jetty!

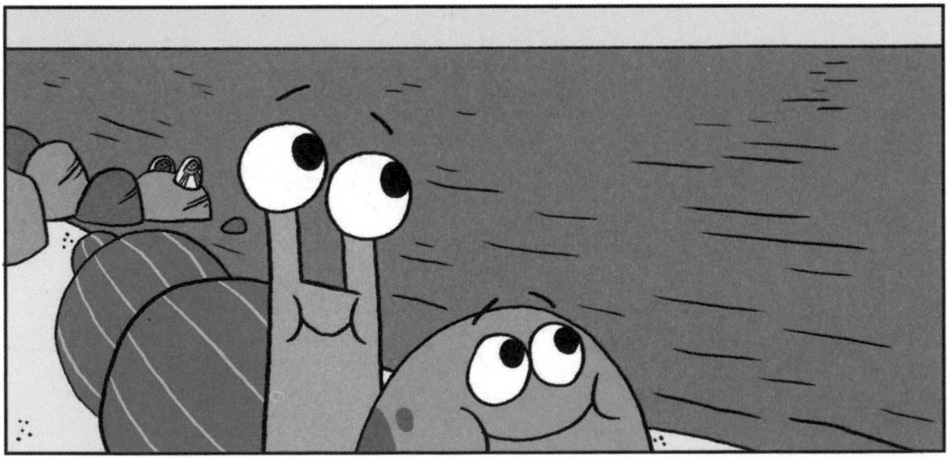

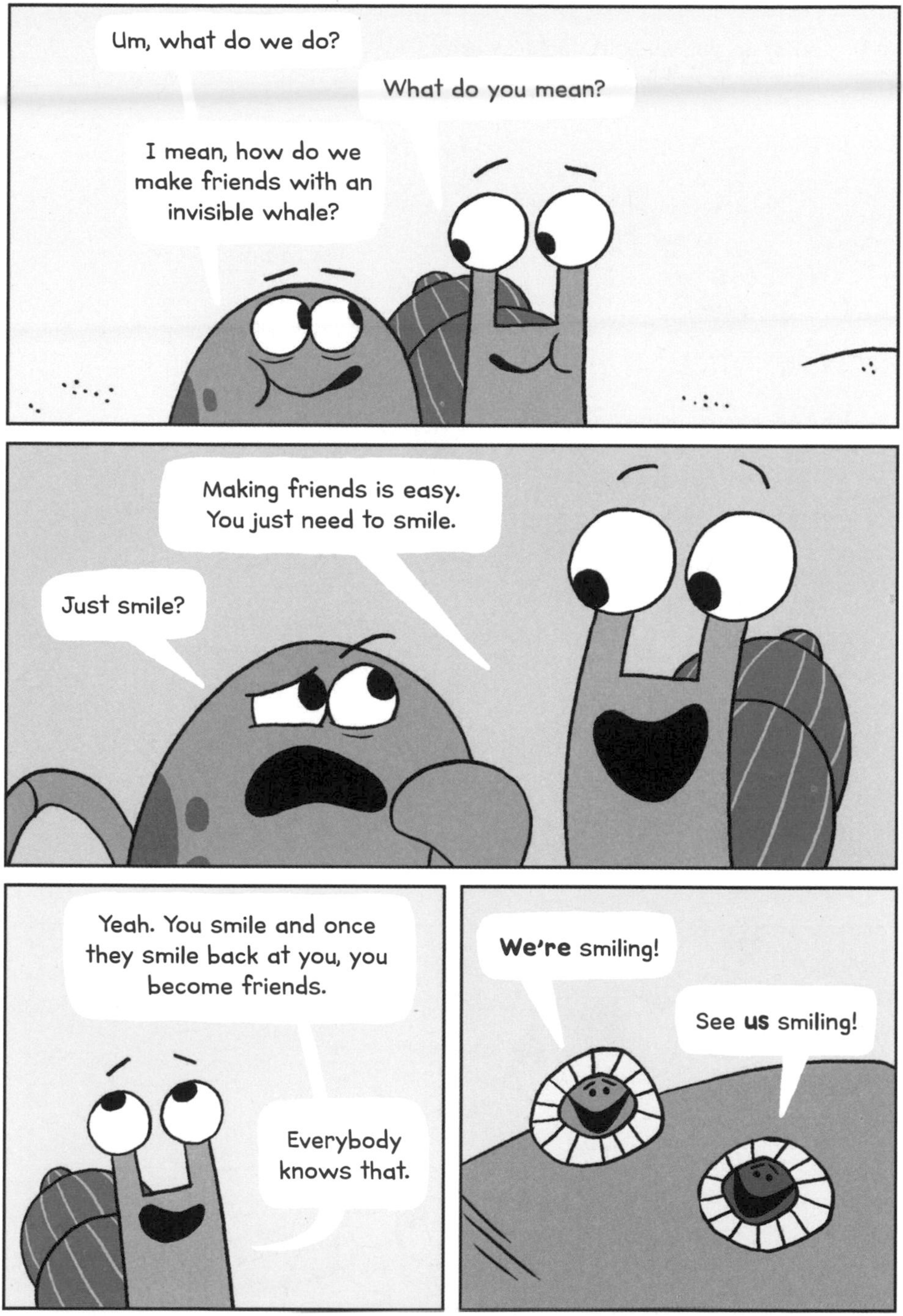

Um, what do we do?
What do you mean?
I mean, how do we make friends with an invisible whale?
Making friends is easy. You just need to smile.
Just smile?
Yeah. You smile and once they smile back at you, you become friends.
Everybody knows that.
We're smiling!
See **us** smiling!

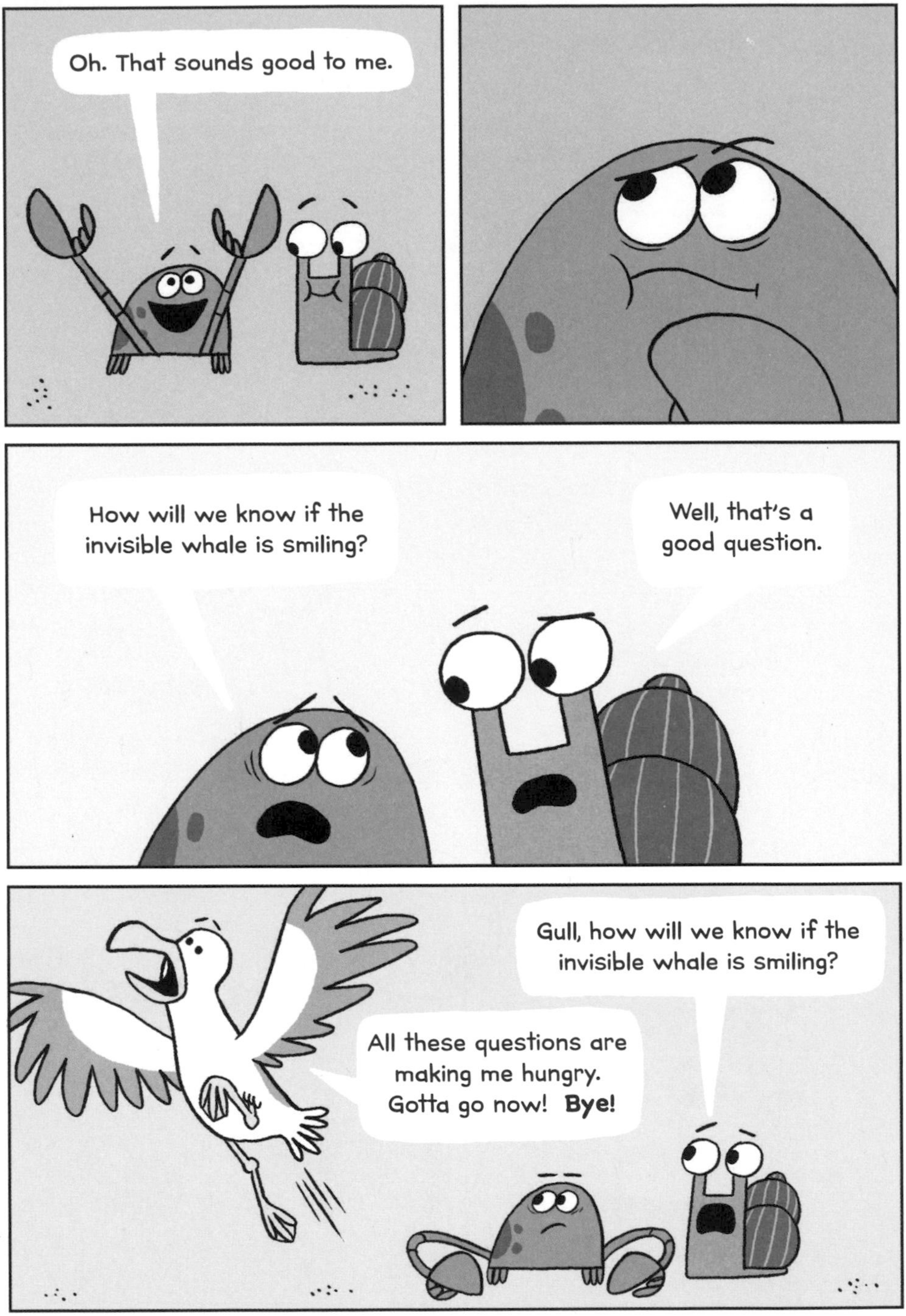
Oh. That sounds good to me.
How will we know if the invisible whale is smiling?
Well, that's a good question.
Gull, how will we know if the invisible whale is smiling?
All these questions are making me hungry. Gotta go now! **Bye!**

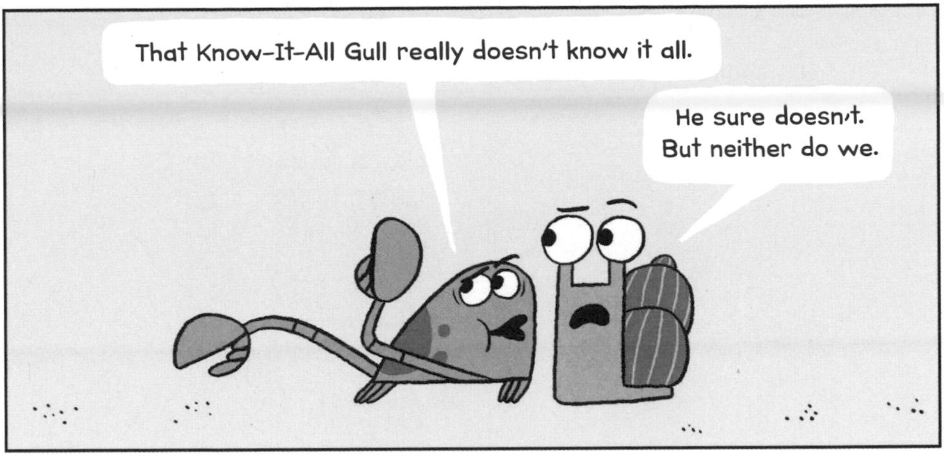
That Know-It-All Gull really doesn't know it all.
He sure doesn't. But neither do we.

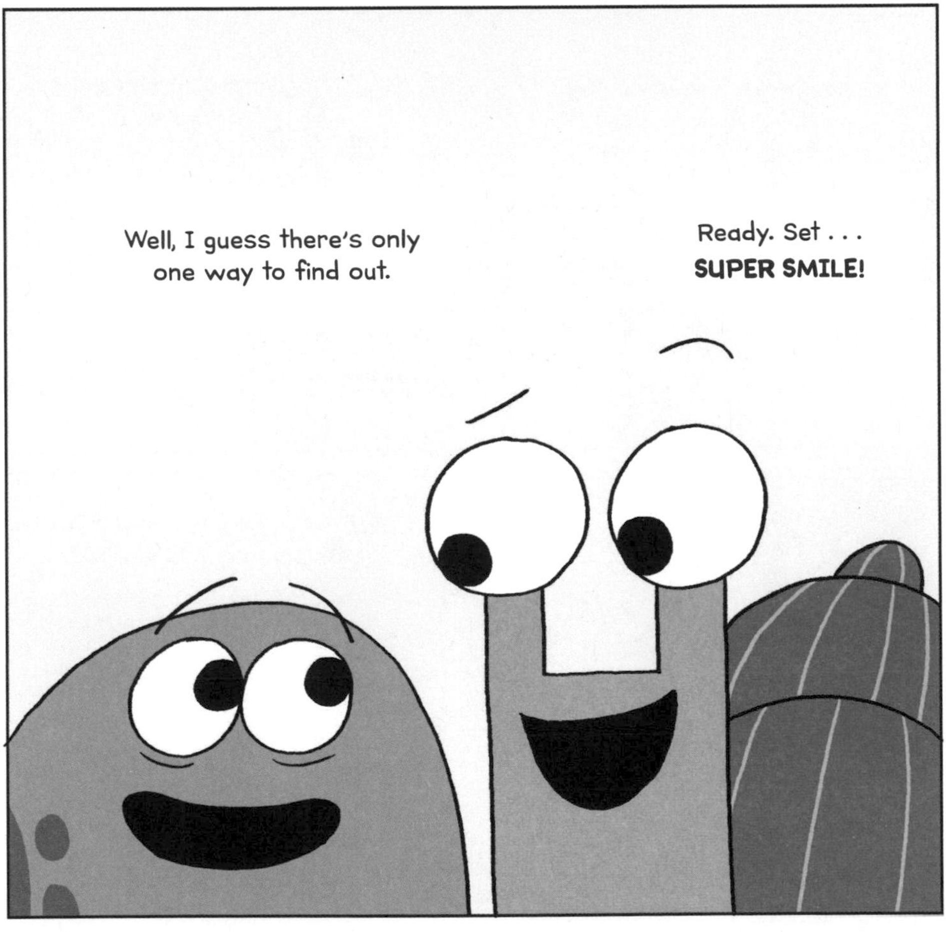
Well, I guess there's only one way to find out.
Ready. Set . . . **SUPER SMILE!**

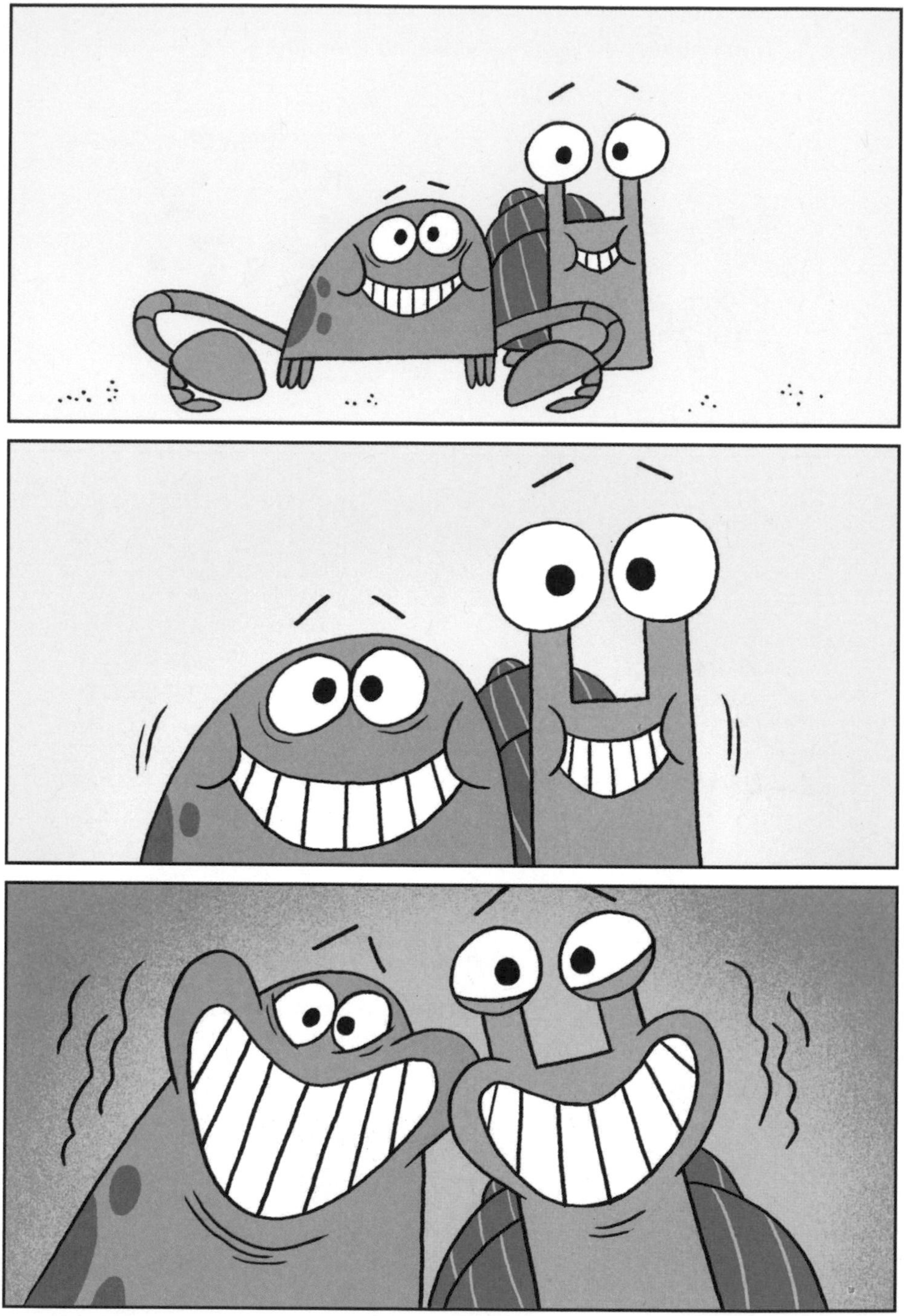

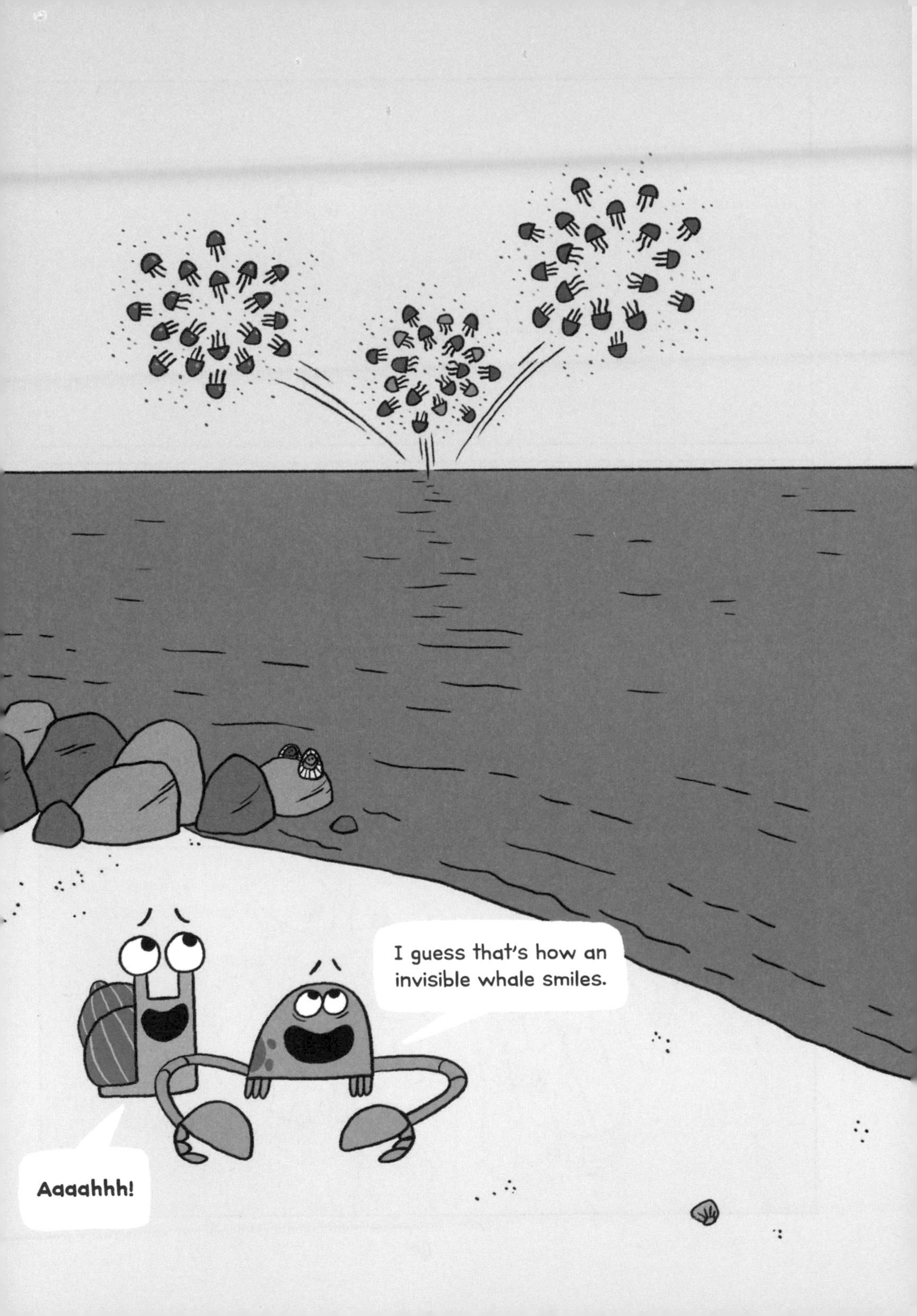
I guess that's how an invisible whale smiles.
Aaaahhh!

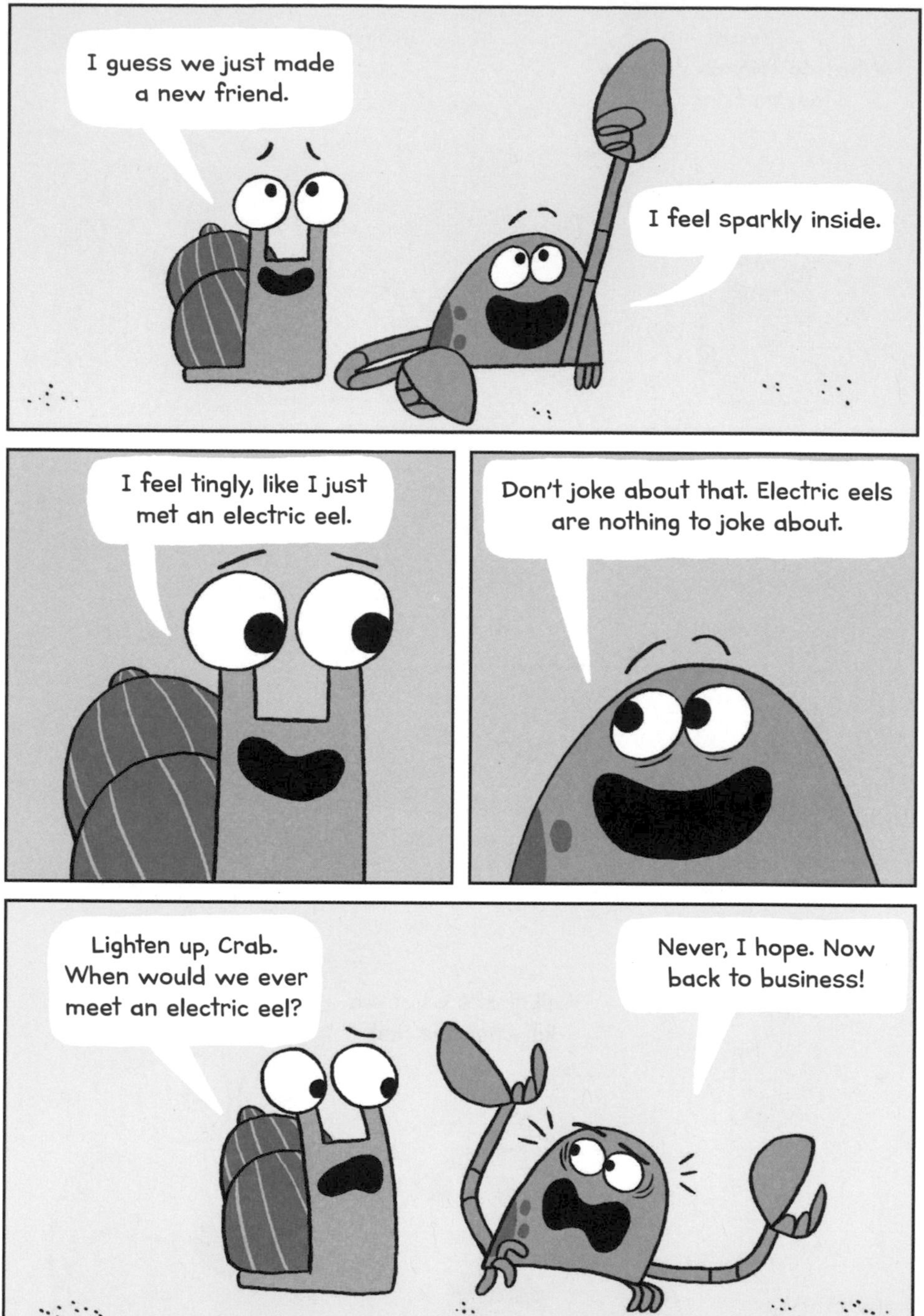
I guess we just made a new friend.
I feel sparkly inside.
I feel tingly, like I just met an electric eel.
Don't joke about that. Electric eels are nothing to joke about.
Lighten up, Crab. When would we ever meet an electric eel?
Never, I hope. Now back to business!

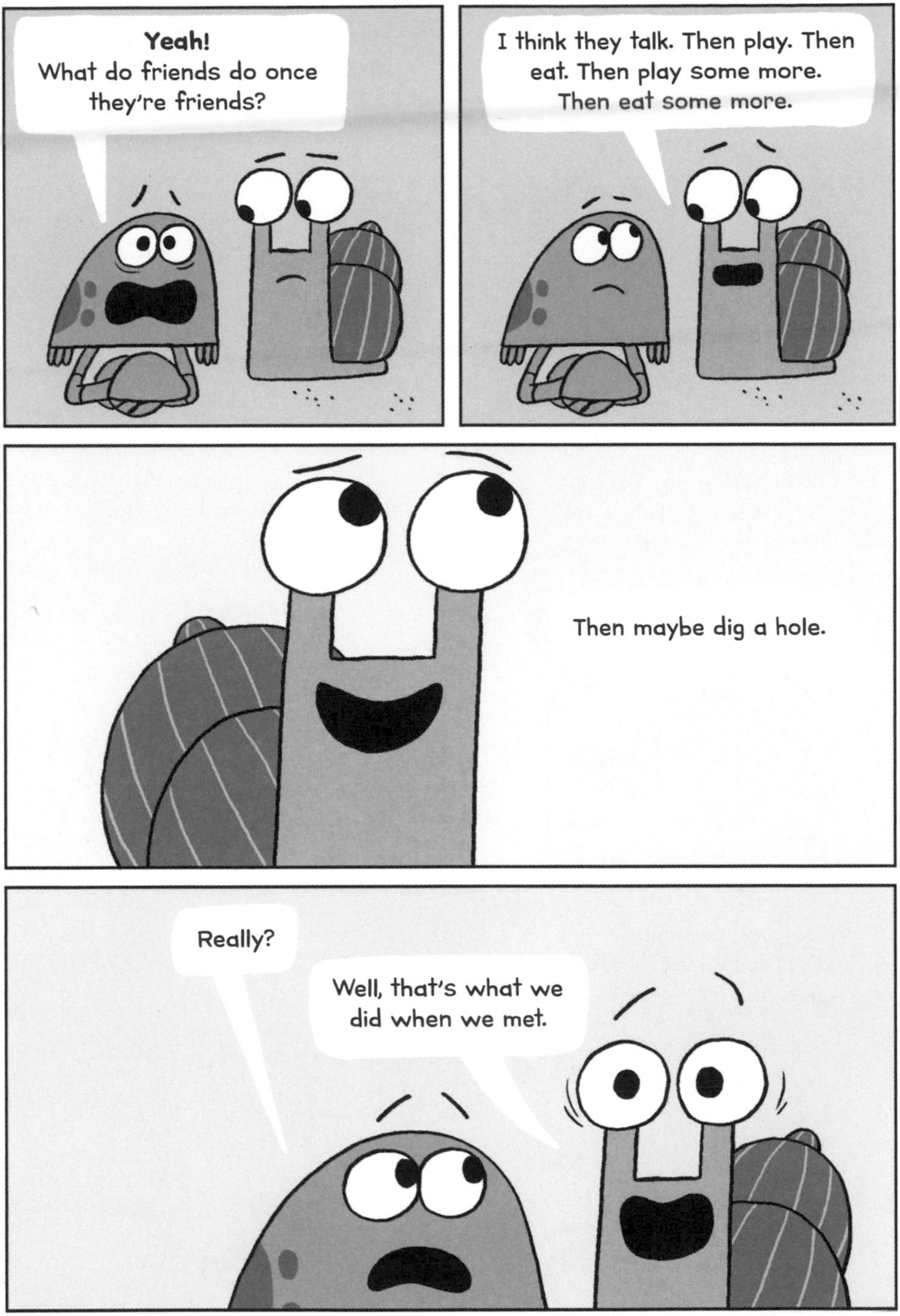
Yeah!
What do friends do once they're friends?
I think they talk. Then play. Then eat. Then play some more. Then eat some more.
Then maybe dig a hole.
Really?
Well, that's what we did when we met.

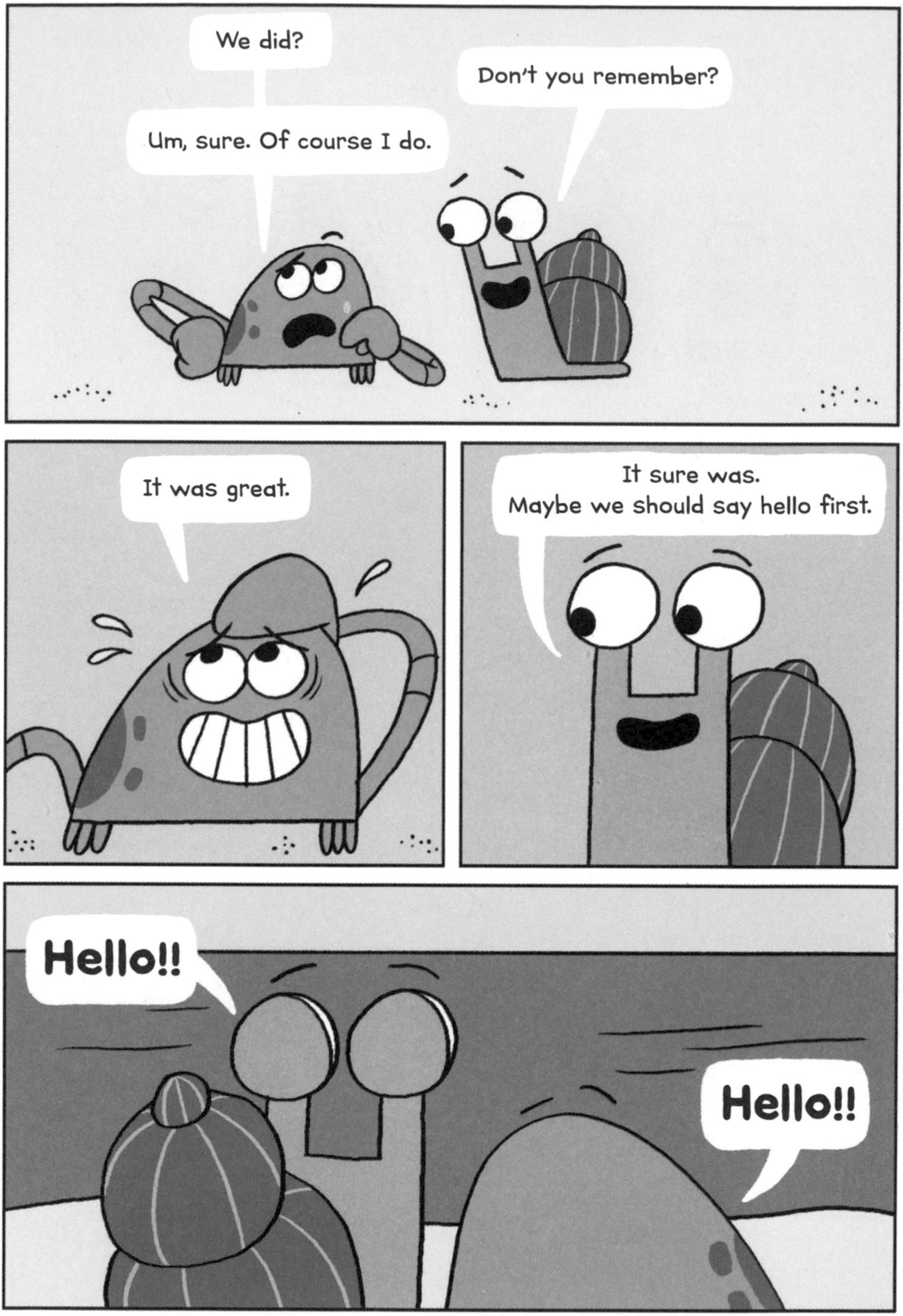
We did?
Don't you remember?
Um, sure. Of course I do.
It was great.
It sure was.
Maybe we should say hello first.
Hello!!
Hello!!

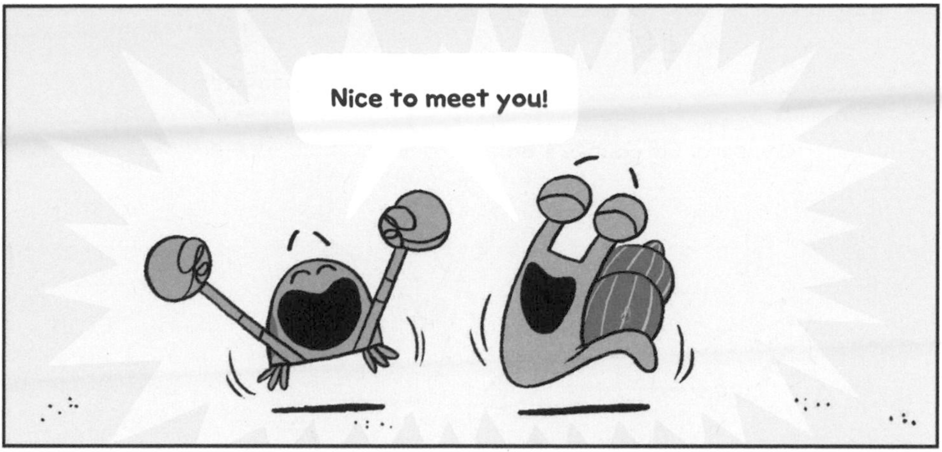
Nice to meet you!

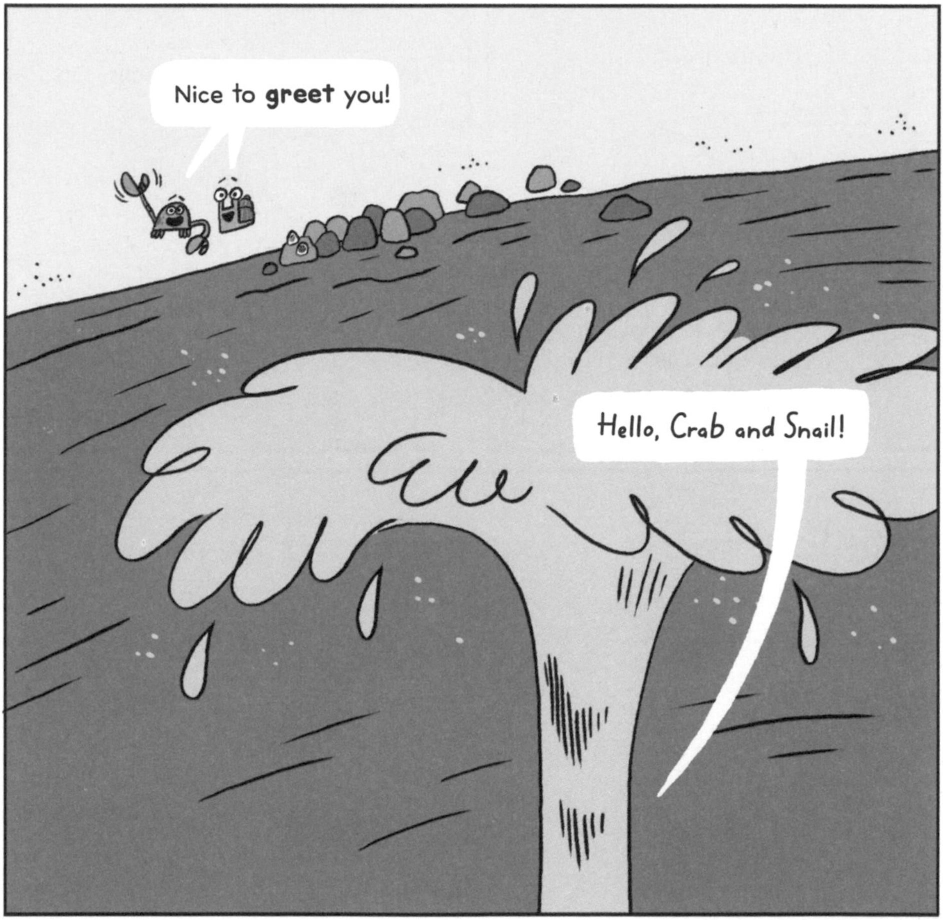
Nice to **greet** you!
Hello, Crab and Snail!

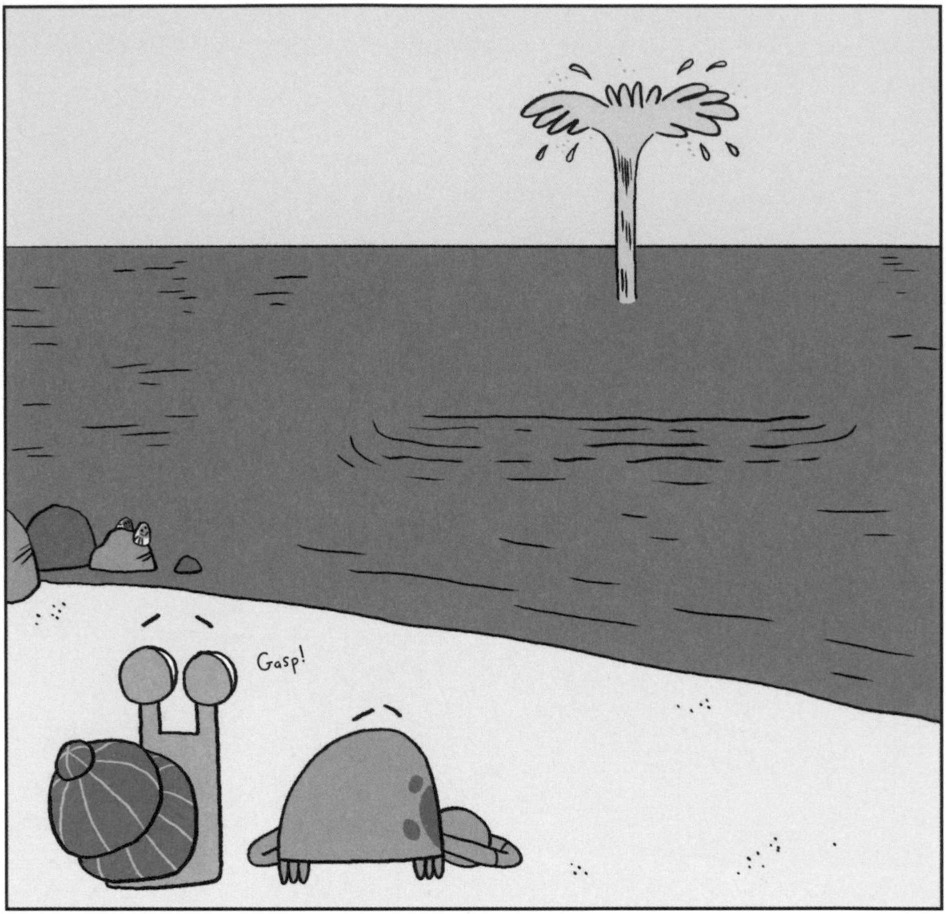
Gasp!

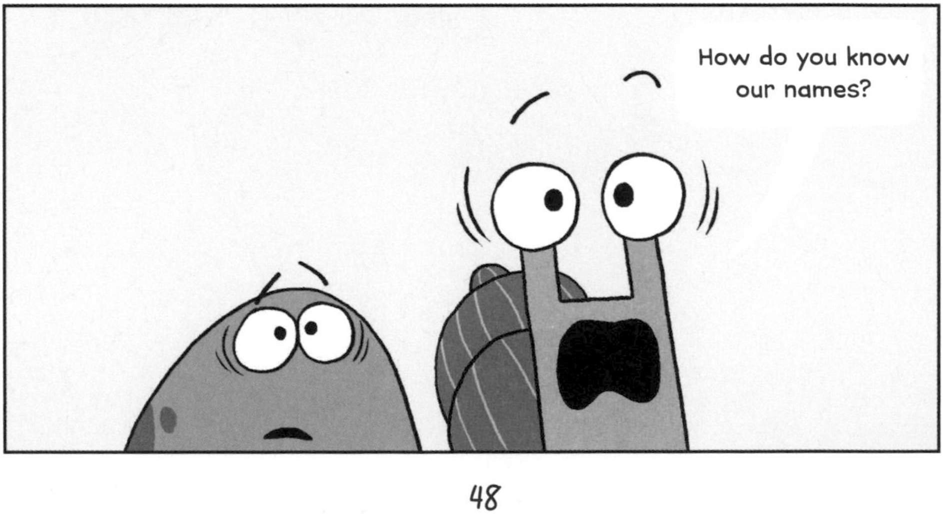
How do you know our names?

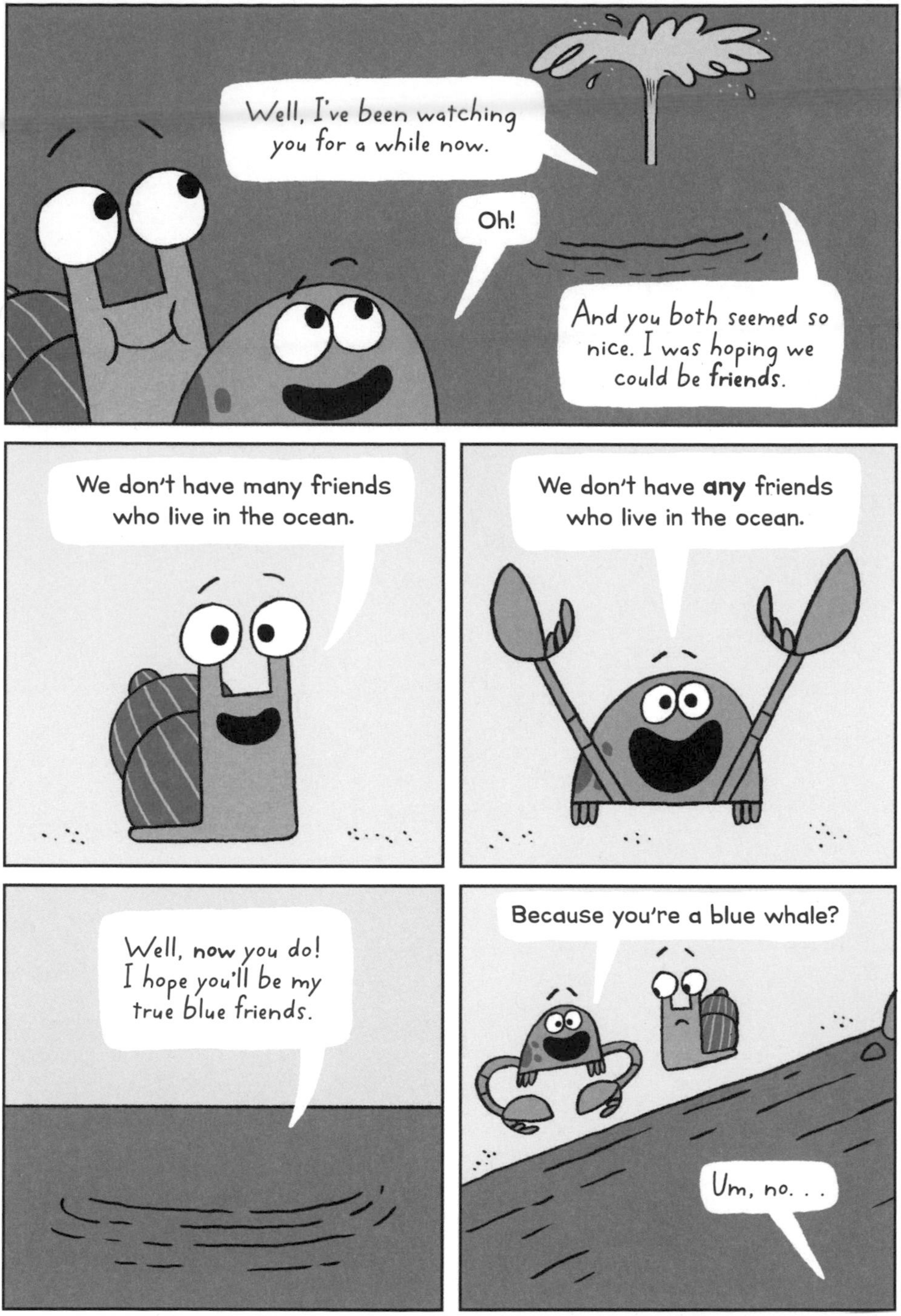
Well, I've been watching you for a while now.
Oh!
And you both seemed so nice. I was hoping we could be **friends**.
We don't have many friends who live in the ocean.
We don't have **any** friends who live in the ocean.
Well, now you do! I hope you'll be my true blue friends.
Because you're a blue whale?
Um, no. . .

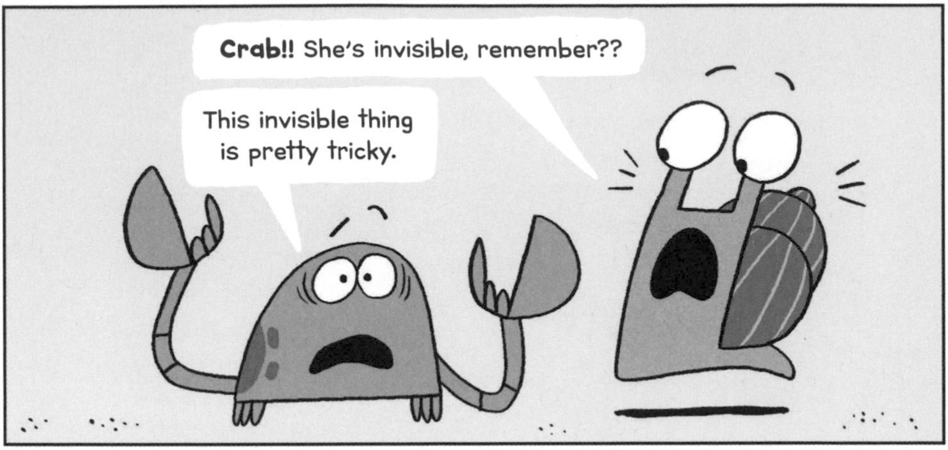
Crab!! She's invisible, remember??
This invisible thing is pretty tricky.

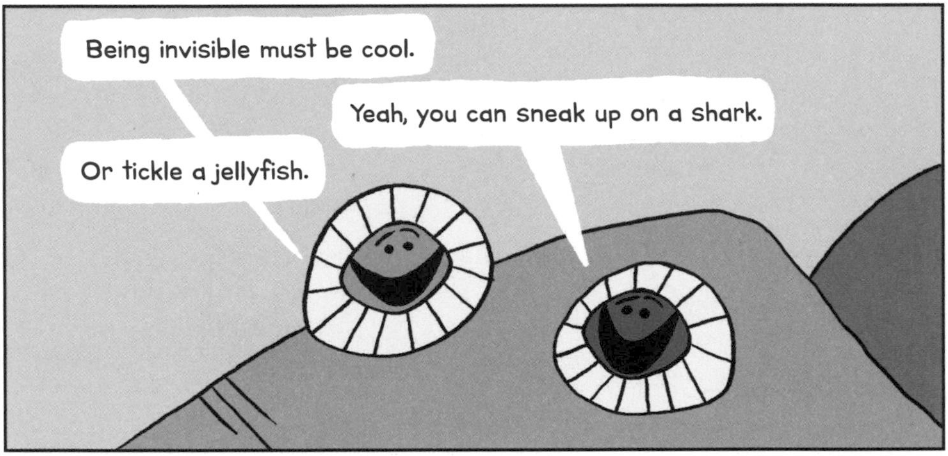
Being invisible must be cool.
Yeah, you can sneak up on a shark.
Or tickle a jellyfish.

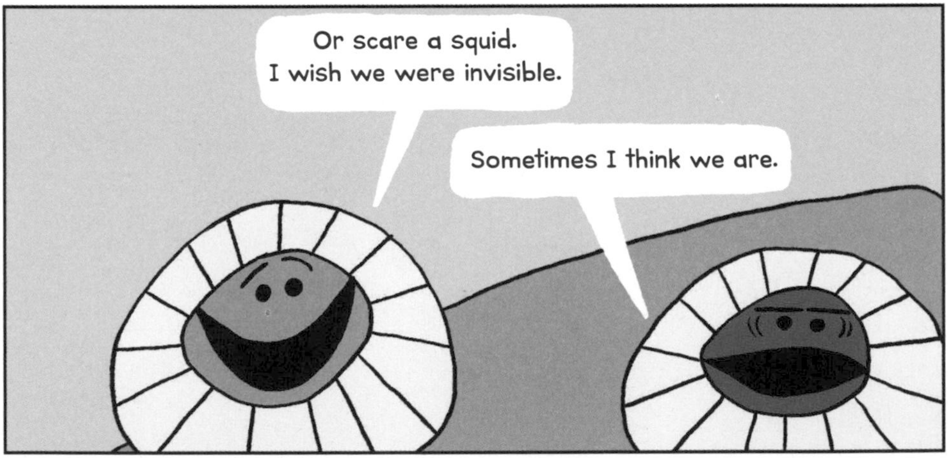
Or scare a squid. I wish we were invisible.
Sometimes I think we are.

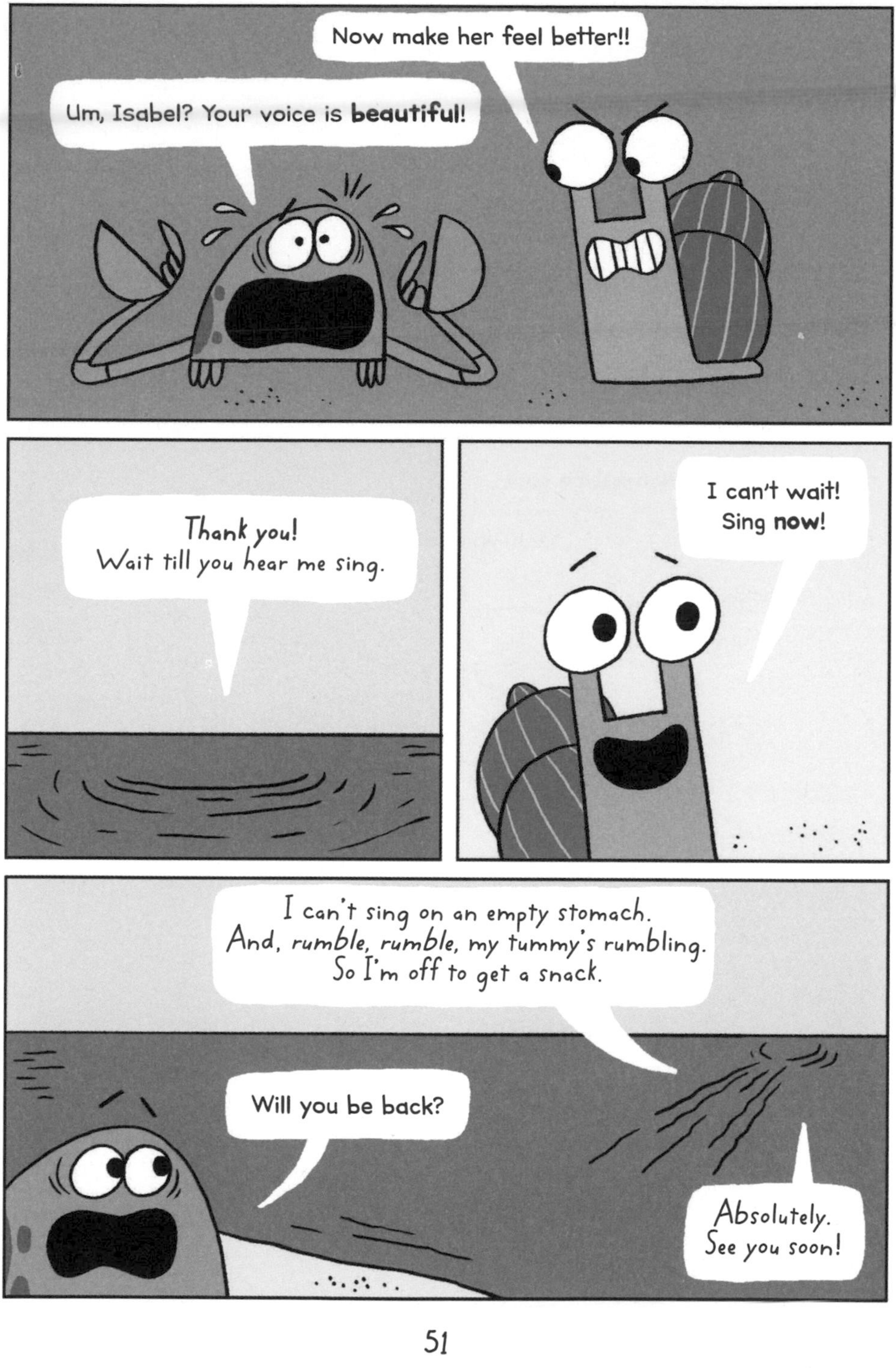
Um, Isabel? Your voice is **beautiful**!
Now make her feel better!!
Thank you! Wait till you hear me sing.
I can't wait! Sing **now**!
I can't sing on an empty stomach. And, *rumble, rumble,* my tummy's rumbling. So I'm off to get a snack.
Will you be back?
Absolutely. See you soon!

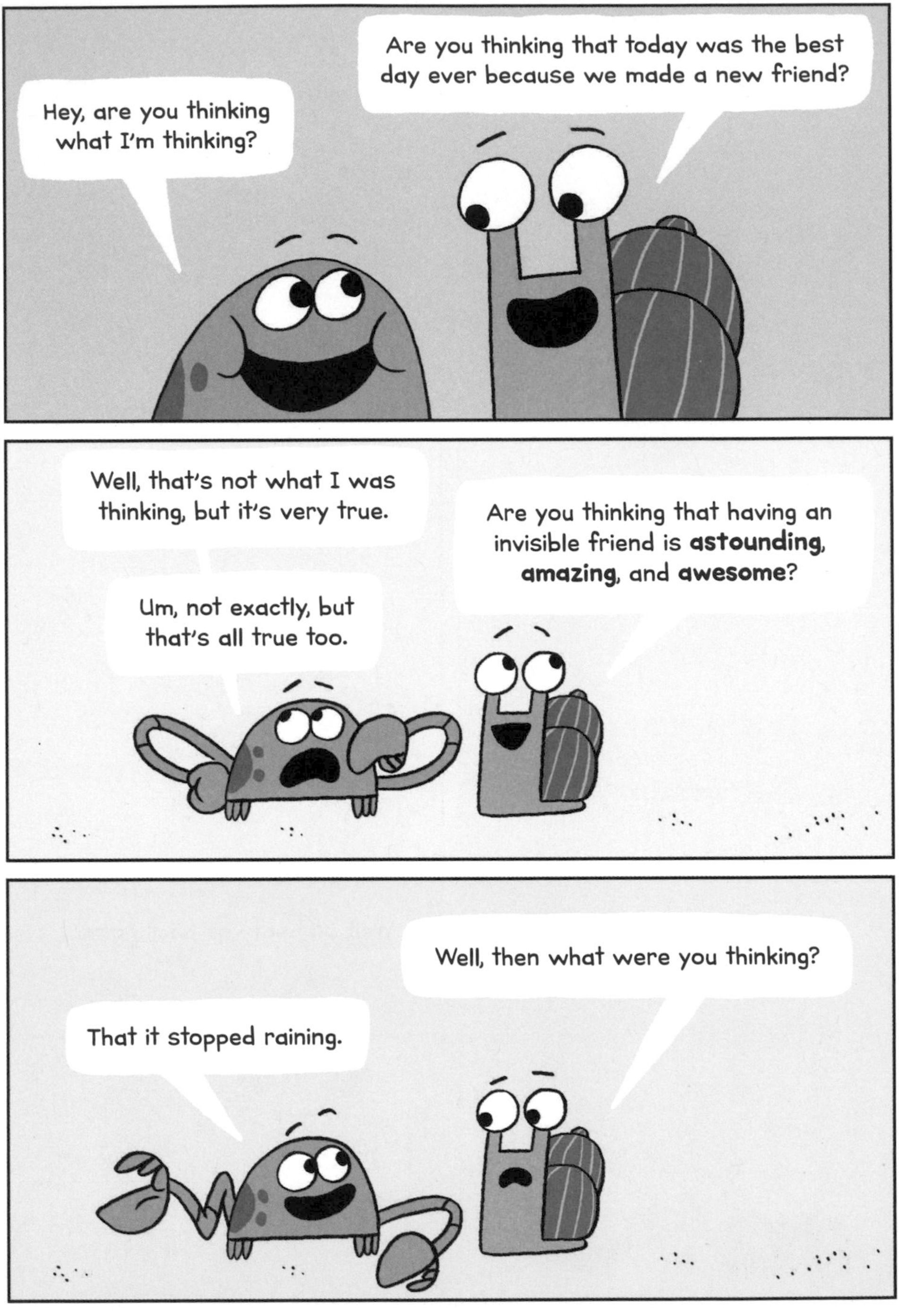
Hey, are you thinking what I'm thinking?
Are you thinking that today was the best day ever because we made a new friend?
Well, that's not what I was thinking, but it's very true.
Are you thinking that having an invisible friend is **astounding**, **amazing**, and **awesome**?
Um, not exactly, but that's all true too.
Well, then what were you thinking?
That it stopped raining.

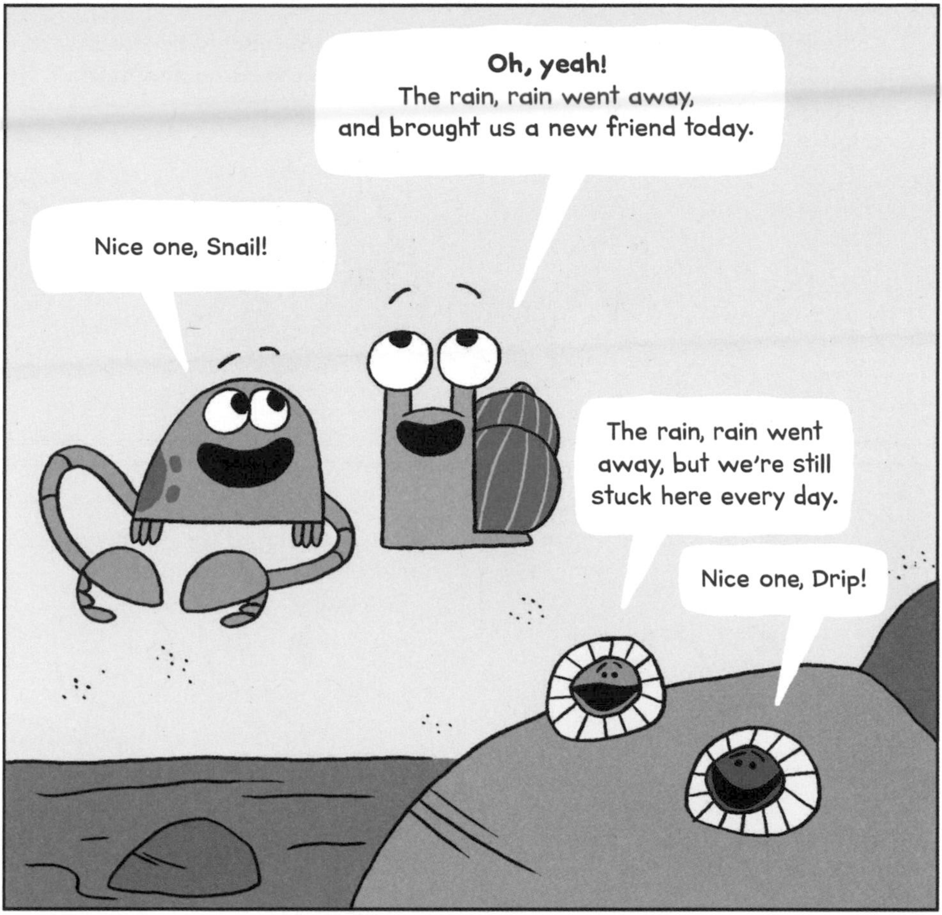
Oh, yeah!
The rain, rain went away,
and brought us a new friend today.
Nice one, Snail!
The rain, rain went away, but we're still stuck here every day.
Nice one, Drip!

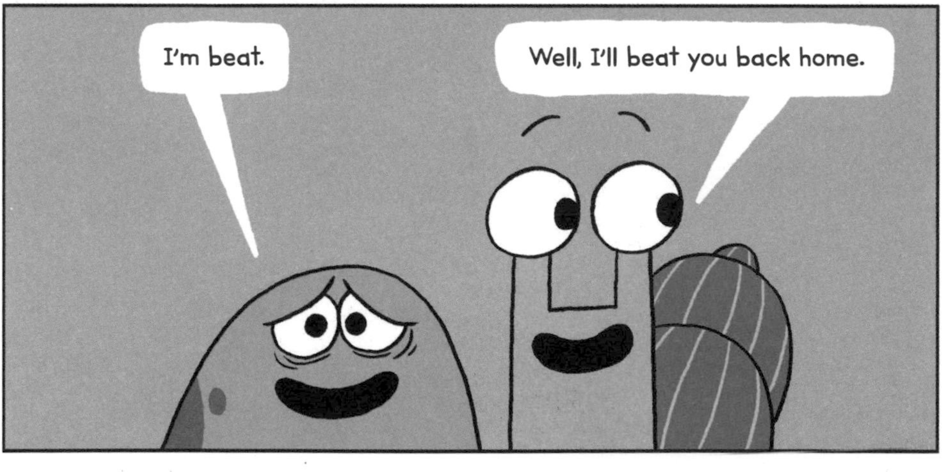
I'm beat.
Well, I'll beat you back home.

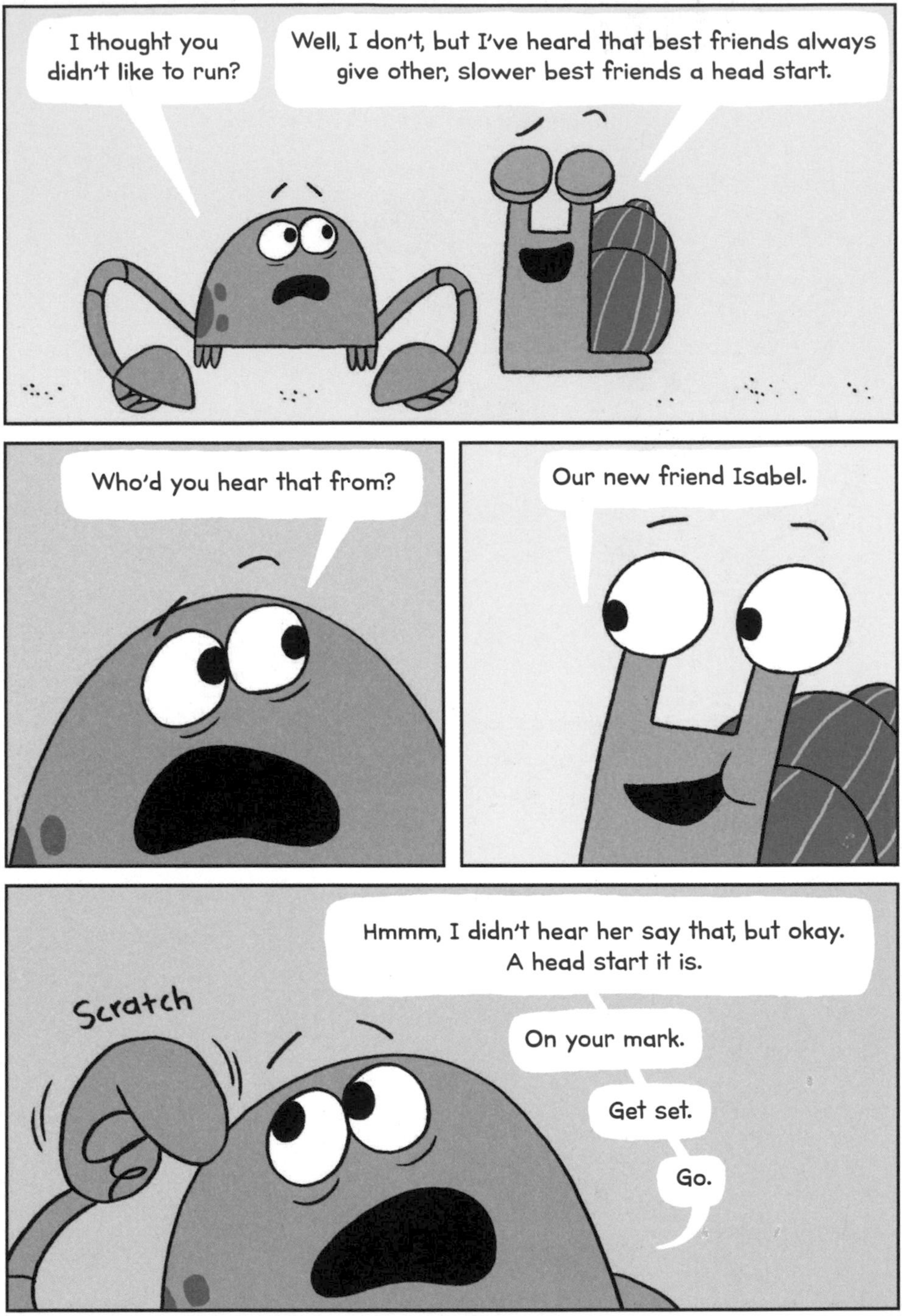
I thought you didn't like to run?
Well, I don't, but I've heard that best friends always give other, slower best friends a head start.
Who'd you hear that from?
Our new friend Isabel.
Hmmm, I didn't hear her say that, but okay. A head start it is.
Scratch
On your mark.
Get set.
Go.

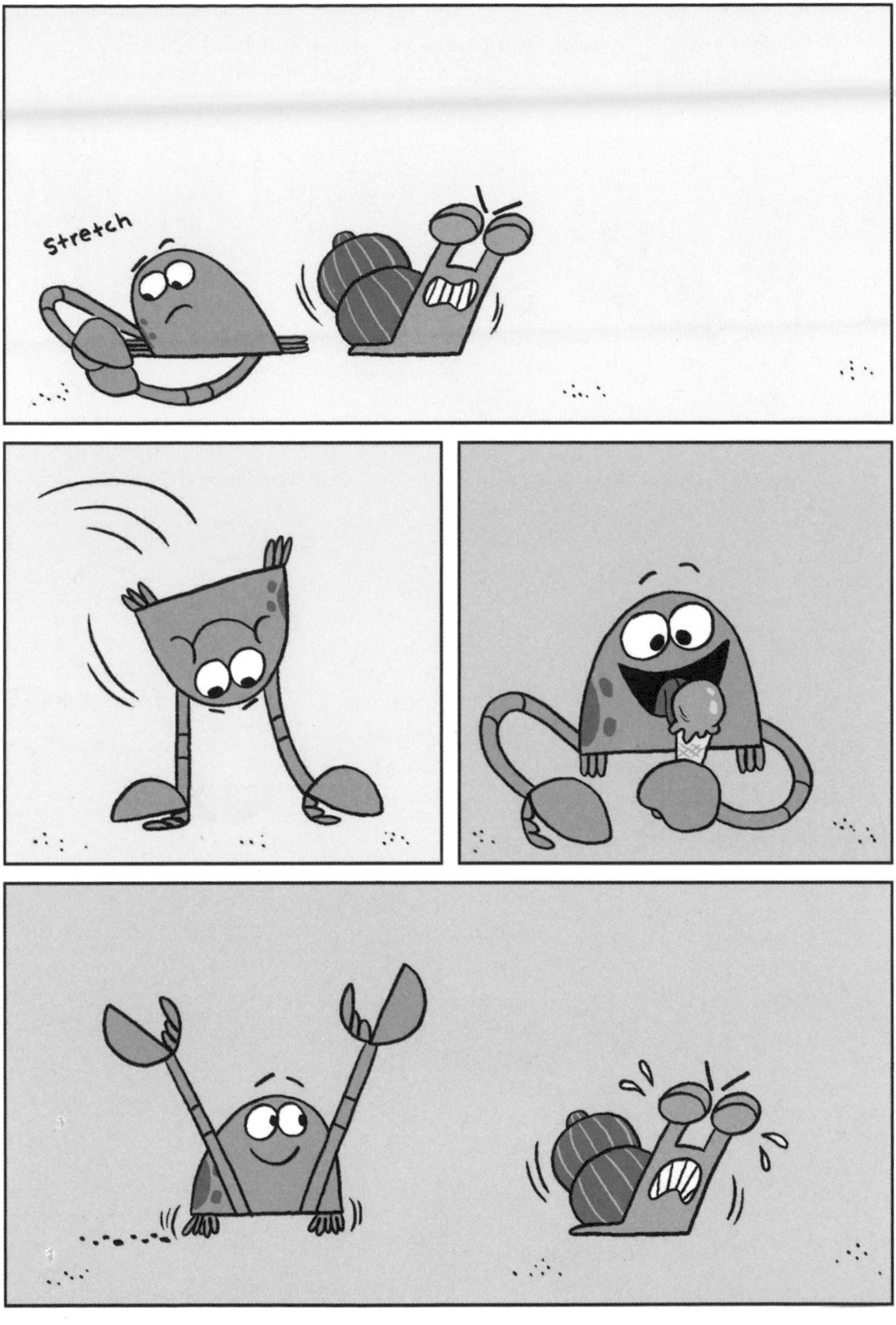
Stretch

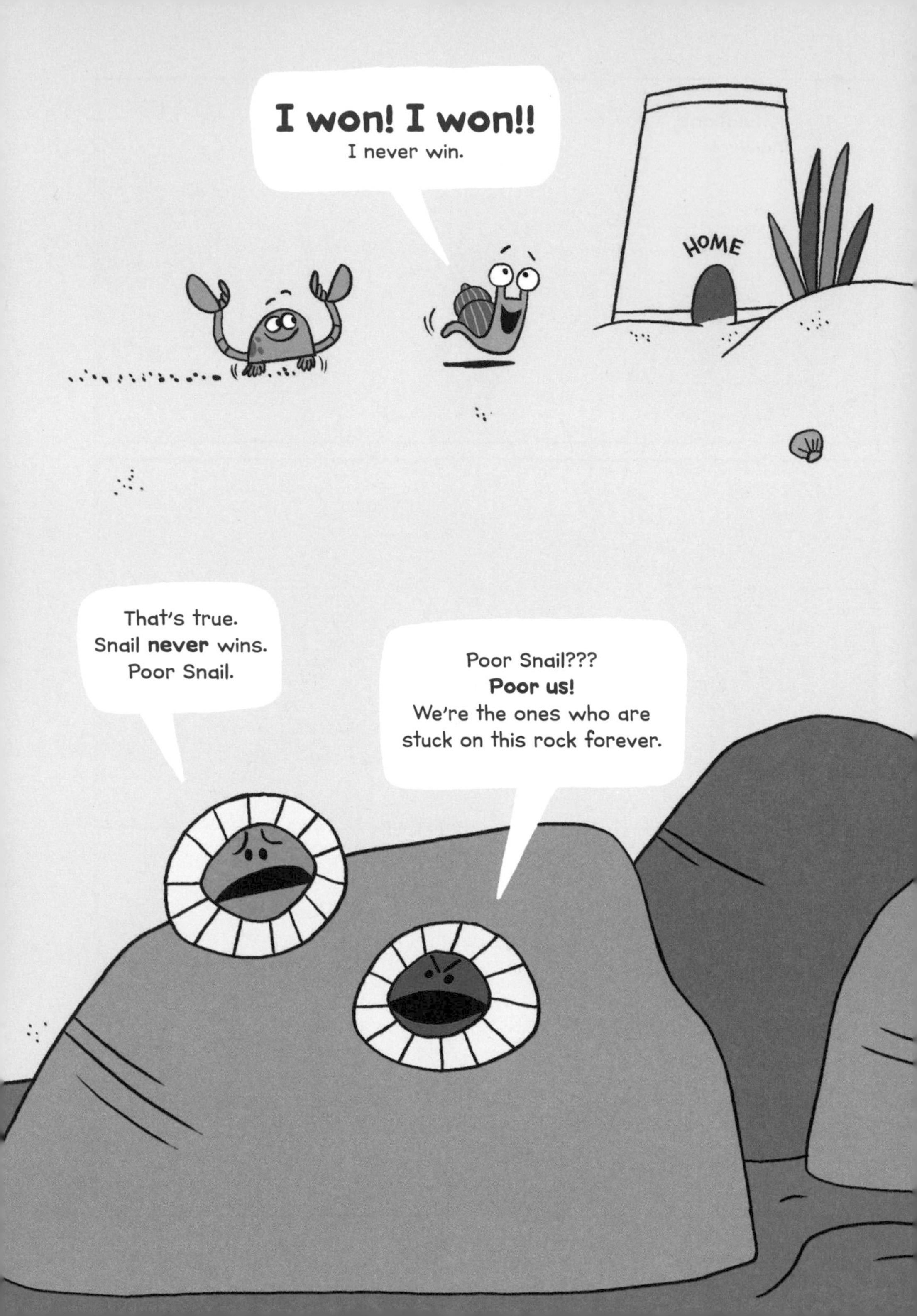
I won! I won!! I never win.
HOME
That's true. Snail never wins. Poor Snail.
Poor Snail??? Poor us! We're the ones who are stuck on this rock forever.

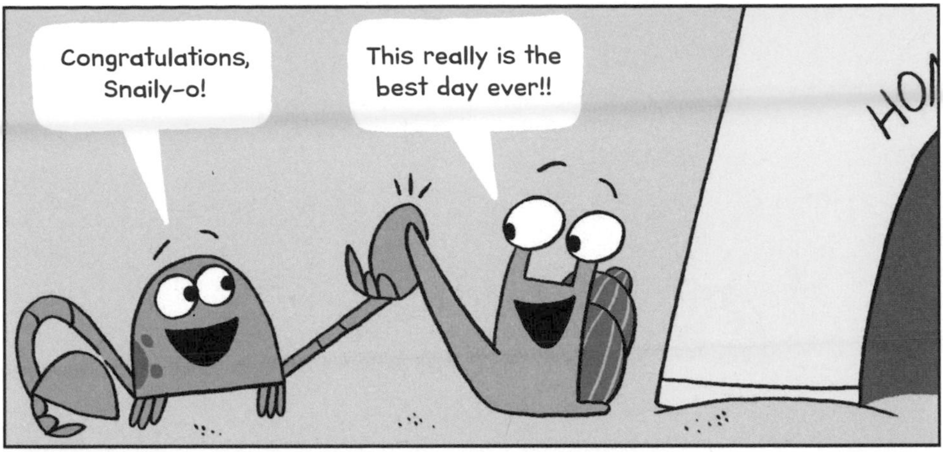
Congratulations, Snaily-o!
This really is the best day ever!!
HO

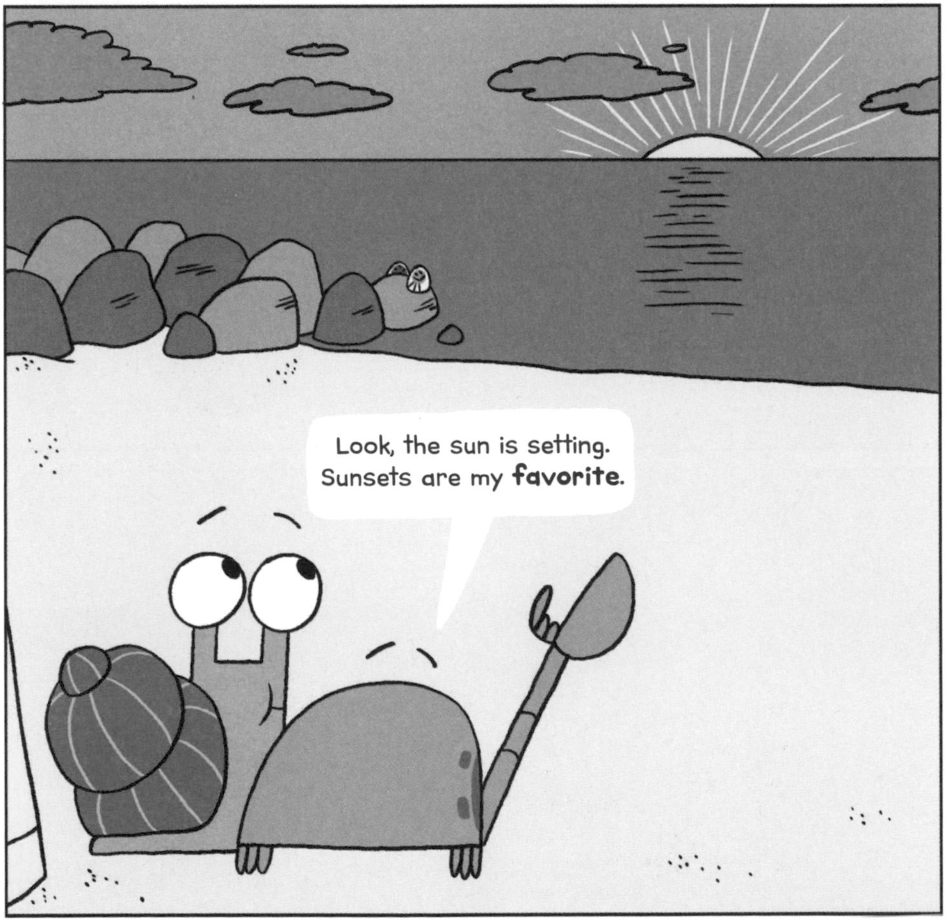
Look, the sun is setting. Sunsets are my **favorite**.

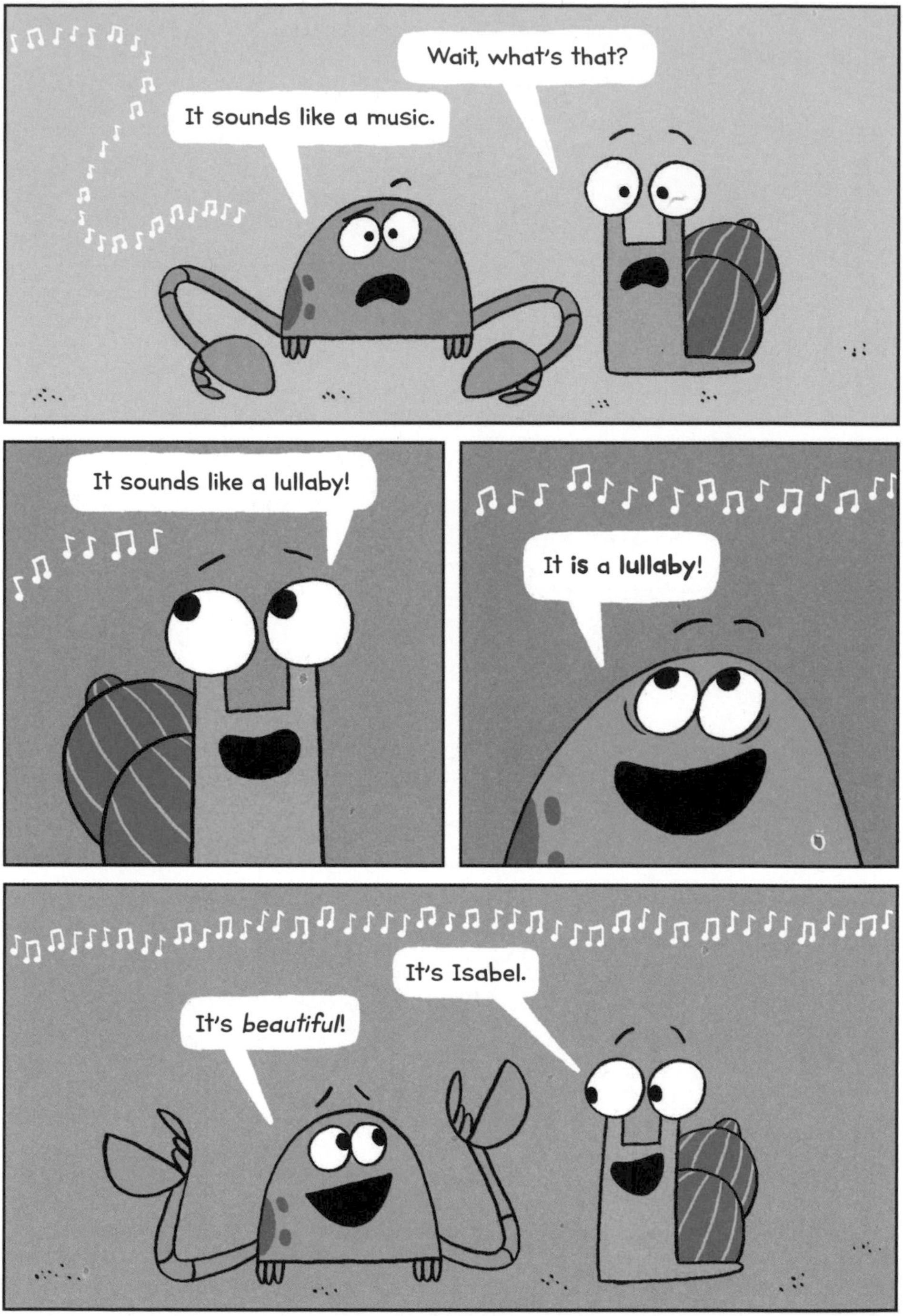
Wait, what's that?
It sounds like a music.
It sounds like a lullaby!
It **is** a **lullaby**!
It's Isabel.
It's *beautiful*!

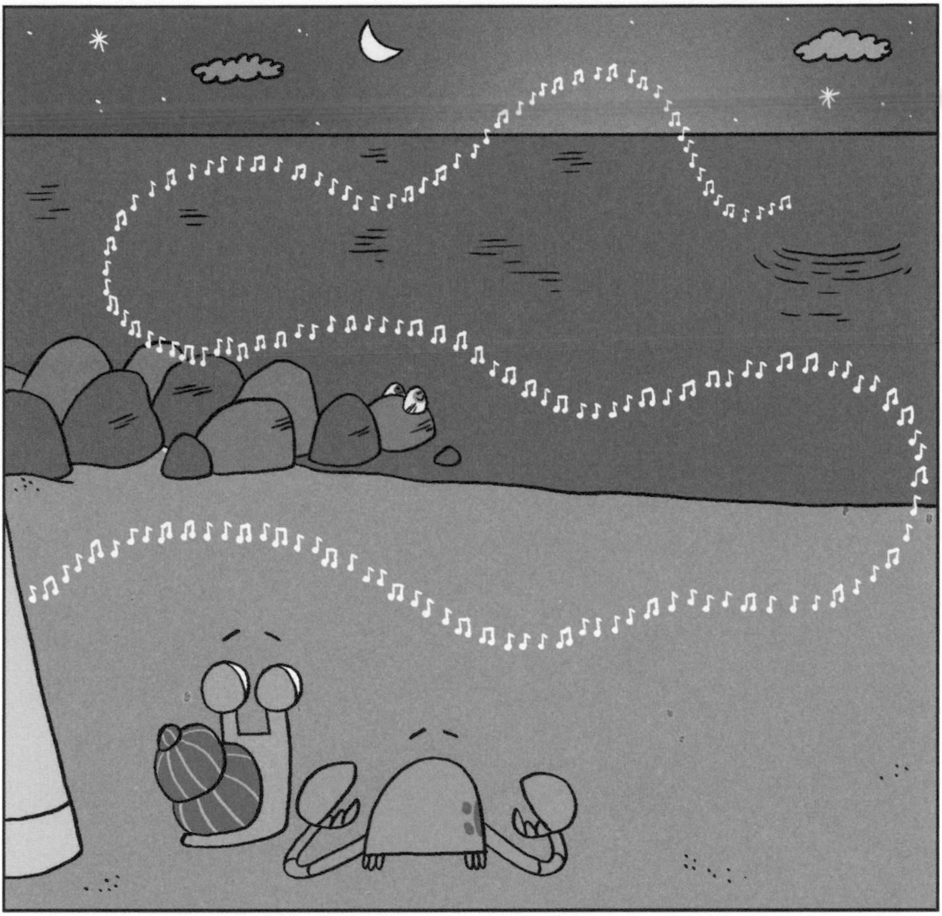

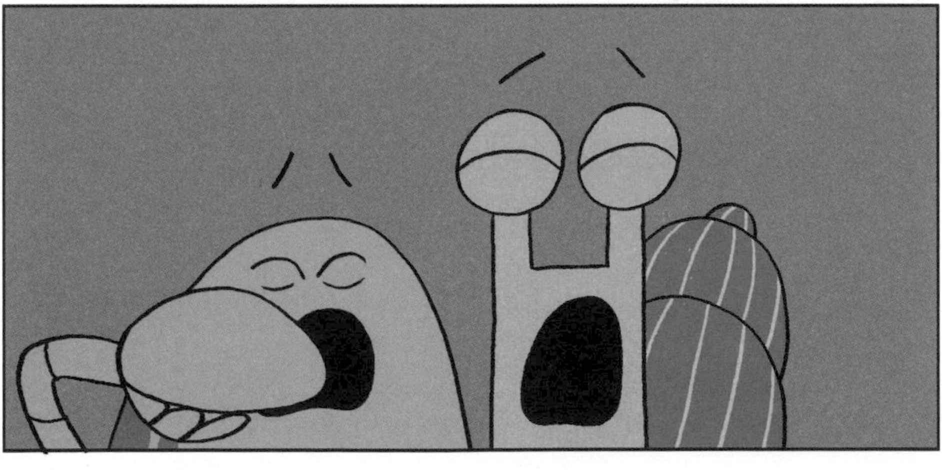

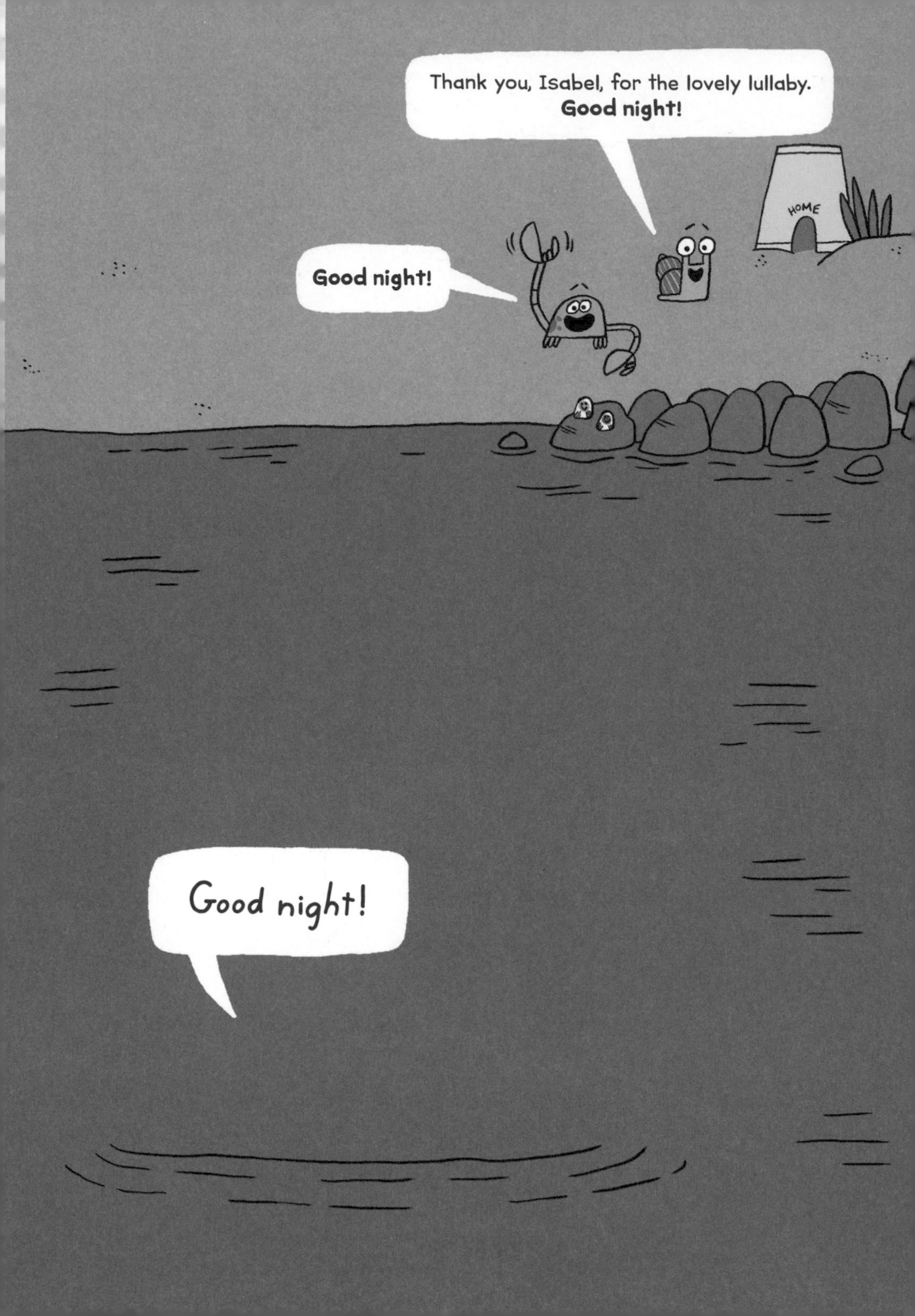
Thank you, Isabel, for the lovely lullaby. **Good night!**
Good night!
HOME
Good night!

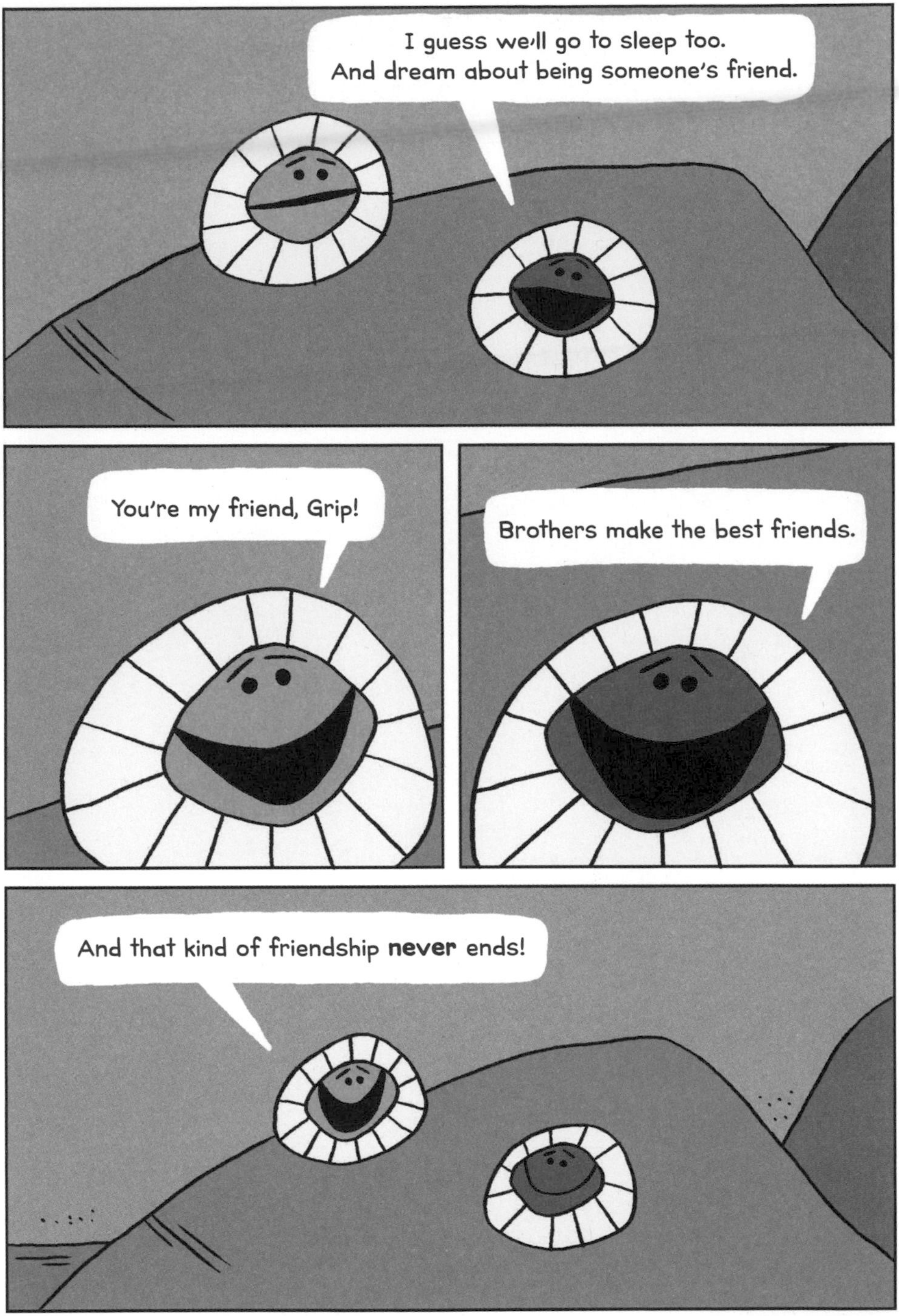
I guess we'll go to sleep too.
And dream about being someone's friend.
You're my friend, Grip!
Brothers make the best friends.
And that kind of friendship **never** ends!

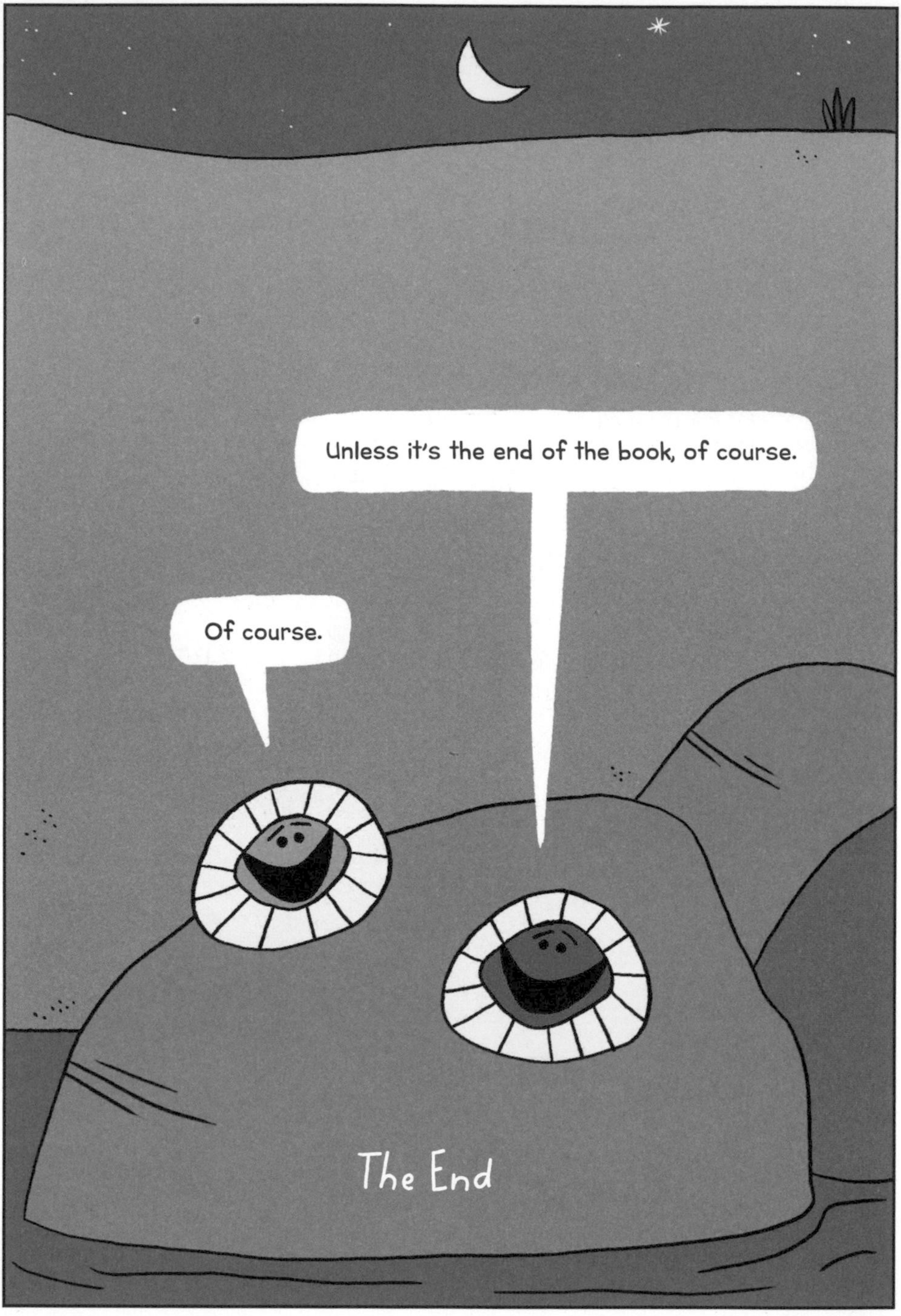
Unless it's the end of the book, of course.
Of course.
The End

Check out more seaside adventures!

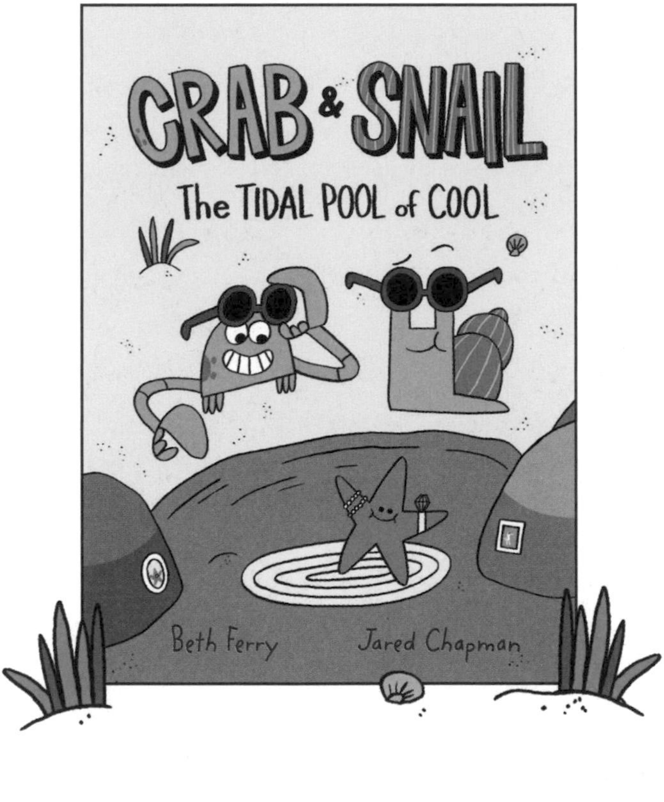
CRAB & SNAIL
The TIDAL POOL of COOL
Beth Ferry
Jared Chapman

Beth Ferry has never met an invisible whale—at least she doesn't think she has. She lives near the beach in New Jersey where she *has* met many a crab and snail, some super-smart seagulls, and more barnacles than she can count. Beth and her family love nothing more than walking along the seashore, looking for interesting and wondrous things. In addition to writing books about the beach, Beth enjoys writing about friendship, nice dreams, and scarecrows. You can learn more at www.bethferry.com.

Jared Chapman is the author and illustrator of books such as *Vegetables in Underwear*; *T. Rex Time Machine*; and *Steve, Raised by Wolves*. When he isn't at the beach looking for invisible sea life, Jared lives with his wife and four kids in Northeast Texas. Visit him online at www.jaredchapman.com.